BROWN

First Edition of 300
APE#039
Published by Art Paper Editions
ISBN 9789490800222

Edited by Emi Kodama and Hou Chien Cheng
Designed by Hou Chien Cheng and Studio Jurgen Maelfeyt
Printed by New Goff
Special thanks to Patrick Ronse, Jurgen Maelfeyt, Emi Kodama,
Mia Verstraete and the Be-Part team

This book has been published with the support of the Executive
of the Provincial Council of West Flanders.

With the support of

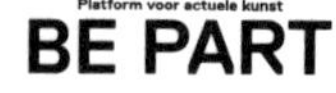

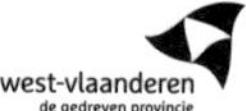

BROWN

HOU CHIEN CHENG

To

Jeff Brown

PART ONE

Marie Vandenberghe

It was a Thursday back in 1991 when I left town. Uncle Wim used to say that a journey should never begin on a Thursday, but the sky was so seductive I could not resist. The funeral on Saturday was beautiful and well attended; I never realized Father had so many friends. After the service I packed my bags and headed to *Antwerpen.* The two-hour train ride seemed like such a courageous thing to do at the age of seventeen. And now, for the first time in years, the much-changed view from that night is playing in reverse outside this train window. I can almost taste the restlessness that is floating in the air.

Hans, the manager of the grocery store, called early in the morning to make sure that I hadn't forgotten our appointment today with the lawyer to sign some legal papers. He greeted me on the telephone, "Good morning, Boss."

In the will of my late Aunt Hilde, she didn't specifically mention what I should do with the store, but I knew it was her life work and that it would be a great disappointment for her to let it end like this. So I decided to take over the store and continue her legacy.

Around noon, Hans came to pick me up. He drives a yellow '92 Chevy. You don't often see this kind of American pick-up truck in West Flanders, but according to him it was love at first sight, and he never thought of switching to other models. I don't really know Hans since he only started working for Aunt Hilde after I moved away. He told me he used to be married, for twelve years, but has now been divorced for five. His wife couldn't bear the loneliness and the constant homesickness any longer. One day she left and never came back. She was a foreigner. They met on the Internet. I didn't say anything when I heard the story. I feel sorry for Hans, but I can understand why she did it, well, at least for the part about feeling isolated in this town. And to think I'm a local. He said it was a good thing they didn't have children. Hans gave me an oh-well-that's-life kind of smile and asked me to take out the paper for the lawyer from the glove compartment. It was then that I saw an envelope from some travel agent lying beneath the paper. I asked Hans if he was going on a vacation, and he told me it was supposed to be a gift to his wife so she could visit her family. But she left a week before he could surprise her.

Hans asked a lot of questions about *Antwerpen* and how it was living there. He said he always wanted to visit but it seemed like such a big fuss, so in the end he never made the trip. I told him he wasn't missing anything, and he told me that it was the city-attitude talking. We both laughed. After the meeting, I told Hans I wished to take a little walk before heading home. He didn't object.

"See you at the store, Boss." Hans said.

The special attention he put on the word *Boss* was almost charming. I sat on the bench by the street for a while. It was then I noticed a well-guarded excitement starting to surface.

Did you know that the day at a grocery store begins at 6 a.m.? I didn't. And apparently if it also runs a bakery it starts even earlier. The concept of being a store owner often appears to be quite impressive when you put it down on paper, and it always seems so simple whenever you read interviews or articles from magazines. But what they don't tell you is the responsibilities behind the title. The grocery store does have its own bakery, but luckily I don't need to run it on my own. Today was my first day being a boss, so I have been up since five this morning getting myself familiar with the day's routine and the staff. They are Hans, his niece Sarah and a part-time worker, Johan. Sarah was born and raised in *Waregem,* and she moved here twelve years ago. Sarah studied philosophy at *Universiteit Gent,* but one day she realized her passion was in baking, and now she is the best baker in town. Johan is local, a typical teenage boy who talks about leaving town all the time and dislikes everything around him. Sarah started working for Aunt Hilde about the same time as Hans, and Johan probably wasn't even born when I left town. It's funny how I'm going to run a store that played a big part in my childhood with people who weren't in it.

Thanks to Sarah, forty percent of the profit comes from the bakery. It's quite intriguing and comforting to know that a good old bakery is still desired and much appreciated. I remember Aunt Hilde used to bring *beuterkoeken* on Sundays when she came by the house after church. Though Mother was never a religious person, and neither were the rest of us, it didn't make Aunt Hilde's visits any less enjoyable. And those *beuterkoeken,* they were wonderful.

I should probably pay Aunt Hilde a visit at her grave, to bring her the good news. Hans told me not to feel bad for not making it to Aunt Hilde's funeral, that missing it wasn't the worst thing in the world. I have never been comfortable when it comes to the death of someone I know. Perhaps no one is, but I have the tendency to act all cold-hearted towards it. I remember in the last year of secondary school, my best friend Sophie's father died. I panicked. It was the first death of someone I knew, someone I used to greet every morning on my way to school. Sophie was so devastated she stayed home for weeks. I didn't comfort her. Instead I cut all contact with her and never spoke to her again. After graduation,

I lost her completely. I wonder how she is. I keep imagining running into her when I'm walking around in town. I guess I'd like to tell her I'm sorry that I acted childish and cruel. But sorry heals nothing I suppose.

The rain is now falling hard on the grass outside in the yard. I can almost see Sophie in the rain, with her yellow umbrella, posing as a much more cheerful version of Mary Poppins.

It didn't snow today like they said it would. I heard the weather forecast on the radio yesterday while driving back after a visit to one of our suppliers. Hope all that trouble of changing to winter tires will pay off later.

Driving somebody else's car is always a strange experience. Sarah was kind enough to lend me hers for the day since the leased car only arrives next week. The car is not new at all, but Sarah keeps her little Sangria Mini so neat it's surreal. Both its exterior and interior are as shiny as the full moon on a dark, dark night. I find the color a bit provocative for a town like this, but I now remember Sarah wears the same shade for her lips. It was the favorite color of her first love, she told me with a big smile on her face when she gave me the key. Purely platonic but they did everything together. One day the family moved away, and she never saw her first love again. Separation seems to be a built-in pattern in life. I wondered.

When I went to return the key, Sarah asked if I'd listened to the CD she'd prepared for my trip. I thanked her and told her how it had made my day when I heard Will Tura's *Ik mis je zo*. It reminded me of my own little first love, a young married man from Macedonia. I met him in a museum in *Oostende*. That was the year before I left town. The exhibition was about the former Yugoslavia. There was this one photograph that made me feel uncomfortable, yet I couldn't stop looking at it.

"You know where this was taken?" a voice asked.

I looked to my left and saw a man. He had short dark hair, a full beard and was wearing a button-down shirt with jeans and a pair of nearly worn-out sneakers. A man who was as normal as could be except for his amber-green eyes that were looking straight at me.

"It was taken in my hometown." The man answered his own question.

This was Mr. J, twenty-six years of age, who came to Belgium with his wife for her to work on a PhD in History. They lived in *Antwerpen* with their two-year-old son. He told me his wife was pregnant again, and this time they hoped it was a girl. They came especially to *Oostende* for the exhibition; his wife thought it might benefit her research.

He told me he enjoyed our conversation and that I was

quite mature for my age. When I told him I should rejoin my friends, Mr. J offered to take me out to dinner that evening since his wife was planning on going to a work event. I said okay. When I think of it now, twenty-six is not old at all, but for a sixteen-year-old girl he was a mystery.

Mr. J managed to get a table at a decent restaurant without a reservation. His fingers touched mine a couple of times between the courses. After dinner, he walked me back to the station. Though I liked him a lot, I wasn't going to ask for his number. Guess I understood I would not see him again. Mr. J asked if he could kiss me. I said okay.

I got on the train, and we never met again.

Today was my first day off. I decided to share this historical day with Aunt Hilde. Aunt Hilde is buried right next to Mother. Looking at the two unremarkable graves made me wonder if any of the stories Aunt Hilde told were true.

When I was a little girl, on Mother's birthdays, we used to sit around the table and listen to Aunt Hilde recount those glorious stories when Grandpa Andre was still alive. Aunt Hilde's near-whisper, storytelling voice always held me captive.

According to Aunt Hilde, Grandpa Andre was a self-made man who ran a pretty successful fishery before the war. Neither Father, Mother nor I had the chance to experience that specific period of time, but Aunt Hilde was very good at drawing pictures with her words for us to understand exactly how *golden* those days were. When Aunt Hilde was a child, the house hosted *black-tie* affairs every other weekend for the employees and the clients. From time to time, the number of guests was somewhere near two hundred. Grandpa Andre wanted nothing but a great time for his guests. The freshest seafood was handled with utmost care and plated on fancy silverware, and expensive wines were properly poured into antique crystal glasses.

Grandpa Andre often gave speeches before the food was served. Aunt Hilde said he was terrible at it, but everyone else thought it was the highlight of the evening. Aunt Hilde wasn't allowed in the rooms where the guests were on those nights, but that definitely didn't stop her from wandering around. She would hang out with the servants in the kitchen tasting desserts. They all loved her, said Aunt Hilde. After the speech, Grandpa Andre would come into the kitchen to check if everything was ready for the guests. Often Grandpa Andre would also find Aunt Hilde hiding in the pantry, but he was never angry at her wandering. Instead, Grandpa Andre would walk Aunt Hilde upstairs and read her one bedtime story. Yes, only one. It was never enough for Aunt Hilde, but Grandpa Andre had his rules. After making sure Aunt Hilde was sound asleep, Grandpa Andre would visit the kitchen one more time and instruct the servants to begin the dinner service.

I once saw an old family photograph inside a book I borrowed from Aunt Hilde. In it, Grandpa Andre is wearing a dark blue custom-made tuxedo with tails, accompanied by a pair of sleek black pointy leather shoes. The tuxedo looked slightly oversize, but I guess it was the fashion back then. I can tell that Grandpa Andre must have been quite a ladies' man. The truth is, he was. Grandpa Andre had three wives. The marriage with his first wife, a farmer's daughter whom he met on a summer job working at a farm, lasted only seven months. She died from a rare genetic disease. Grandpa Andre was heartbroken. And for that reason, I've never once heard anyone in the family mention her name.

Grandpa Andre met his second wife while he was on holiday on the coast of *Oostduinkerke*. Her name was Josephine, the daughter of a wealthy fisherman, the mother of Aunt Hilde. Although the family was rich, Josephine hated being treated like a princess. On the day she met Grandpa Andre, Josephine was on horseback, in her work clothes, shrimping. She yelled at Grandpa Andre who was by the water reading Guido Gezelle's poems and was in her way.

"Not really the weather for reading outside, is it?" Josephine said. "I mean, with the wind, the rain and the fact that it's February."

"How do you even know I speak *your* language?" Grandpa Andre looked up and responded.

"You are reading Guido Gezelle," Josephine explained while getting off her horse.

"Hasn't anyone ever told you not to judge a book by its cover?" Grandpa Andre got up and looked straight into Josephine's eyes.

"Are you trying to be charming or a jerk?"

Grandpa Andre waited for Josephine to finish her sentence before asking her out. I didn't think Grandpa Andre was being original, but Aunt Hilde thought that was the most romantic encounter she'd ever heard.

People used to talk, saying that Grandpa Andre's success was because of Josephine's family fortune. But the fact is, Josephine's parents were against her marrying him, and when she did anyway they disowned her. Grandpa Andre never took a penny from her family.

Josephine took ill when Aunt Hilde was nine. Aunt Hilde admitted that Grandpa Andre was not a model husband during her mother's illness. He was always caught up in his work and was never home. It was only when Josephine was on her deathbed that Grandpa Andre realized he was going to lose her forever. Aunt Hilde said that was the only time she ever saw her father cry.

When Aunt Hilde was eleven, Grandpa Andre met Grandma Katrien, Mother's mother, a local farmer's daughter. Unlike some cliché soap opera, there was no drama between Grandma Katrien and Aunt Hilde. They hit it off from the very beginning. The next year, Mother was born.

In the following years, Grandpa Andre's business kept on growing. Aunt Hilde remembered that whenever school held a charity event, she was always the first student that teachers asked to make a donation. It was like an obligation. Aunt Hilde said it with an annoyed expression on her face, but deep down, as a child, she had been proud of it. As Aunt Hilde got older, her stories always ended with how she used to have three maids to bathe her or that the girls in school always giggled when the handsome young driver dropped her off at school. I have seen a photograph of that driver and he was not that handsome.

Mother, on the other hand, was never old enough to really experience any of those luxuries. Two weeks after Mother's fifth birthday, Grandpa Andre and Grandma Katrien died in a car crash. Grandpa Andre's accountant was not an honest man, and he somehow managed to steal all of Grandpa Andre's fortune after the tragedy. He even took away the house that Aunt Hilde and Mother grew up in.

Soon the war broke out. Logic didn't seem to apply anymore at the time. Aunt Hilde was barely seventeen, left with nothing, but she bravely faced reality. Usually this would be where Aunt Hilde found it hard to continue her stories. Though she often picked them up again after a while, it wasn't before she'd recalled every sighting of ghosts in the old house. Mother enjoyed both kinds of stories in equal measure. For me it was the perfect timing for a bathroom break.

"So, where was I?" Every time, Aunt Hilde would continue by asking the same question, but she never needed any reminders. She knew exactly where she was. After losing her parents and everything else, in order to survive and take care of Mother, Aunt Hilde dropped out of school and found a temporary job washing dishes. When Mother was eight, Aunt Hilde met a man and got married. But they argued about

Mother a lot, and the following June the man divorced Aunt Hilde.

In her will, Aunt Hilde also left me an old suitcase. I haven't had the time to go through the things in the attic, but I remember Aunt Hilde once mentioned a suitcase in one of her stories. When they were ordered to move out of the old house, Aunt Hilde managed to keep a beautiful suitcase made of calfskin. It was given to her by Grandpa Andre. Though it's quite valuable, Aunt Hilde never thought of selling the suitcase. Not even in desperate times. Inside the suitcase were three dresses Josephine had made for Aunt Hilde. Each dress was tailor-made, and of different fine fabrics. They were made of Indian silk decorated with lace from *Brugge,* vintage hand-dyed wool from *Ieper* and a splendidly embroidered French cotton floral. Aunt Hilde got them between ages five to eight so they didn't fit her anymore, but she kept them for sentimental reasons. Every now and then when she felt life had paralyzed her, Aunt Hilde would stare at those dresses and try to navigate back to the happy times. I used to ask Aunt Hilde why her stories were never about the war. Not one bit. I told her I found it odd.

"It's war. People died. What's there to talk about?" Aunt Hilde would sigh and respond.

That is the kind of person Aunt Hilde was. She preferred to remember the things that made her smile. Before leaving, I whispered to Aunt Hilde's grave, telling her that her store was now in good hands. I thought that should put a smile on her face.

I'm staying at Aunt Hilde's place for the moment. If you knew her, you would see that everything Aunt Hilde owned was a representation of her. It's nice to have her things around. This morning the coffee maker chose to retire. Its bottom was leaking. I was quite upset since it was one of those old-fashioned Italian coffee makers, one that consists of a metal pot with a chamber at the base. You place it on the heat to make coffee. It takes a little longer, but the result is very rewarding. I rang Hans around eight, asking for some tips. I was determined to solve this coffee crisis.

On the telephone, Hans recommended a nice store next to where he lived that sold coffee machines. He said that they didn't open before eleven though, so if I needed some decent coffee at this hour, there was a café he sometimes went to called Sokoke in *Oudenburg*. It just opened a year ago. The owner spent a few years in Kenya and really knew African coffee. Hans said he wasn't sure why the owner chose *Oudenburg*, but the coffee there was good. Normally I'm quite skeptical about cafés I don't know, but since it wasn't far away and since its exotic name was somehow already earning my interest, I decided to give it a go.

It was a quarter past nine when I arrived at Sokoke. There was already one customer in the café, a woman in her late fifties who was wearing a colorful jacket paired with a pink scarf wrapped around her neck and had a hairdo from the seventies. She was on the phone. The café wasn't too small, but there were only two tables: one four-person table and one two-person table. I waved at the woman as I walked towards the two-person table, but she didn't seem to notice me. There was a pile of menus on the two-person table. It looked like the café was still being prepared.

"Good morning, Miss," a gentle, mature voice greeted me with a local accent. I turned around and saw a lean, tall man in a grey sweater behind the bar drying a coffee cup. Although both his hair and beard were as white as snow, something told me he was probably no more than fifty. The man put down the cup and walked towards me with the towel in his hand.

"Good morning," I greeted him back. He removed the menus from the table and took my order. I didn't even read the menu. I just ordered something off the board. It was a Coffee Sokoke.

"You will love it," he said with a subtle confidence as he walked back to the bar. Safe to say, I was charmed by both the café and its owner in an instant. *But why only two tables,* I wondered. While I was waiting for my coffee, I looked over at the four-person table. The woman was still on the phone. Her concentration was unbreakable. But I noticed that she was not talking – in fact, I don't think I heard her talking at all the entire time she was on the phone. For some reason, I began to feel uncomfortable. Looking at her felt like I was caught near an event horizon. Any longer and I'd be sucked in and ripped apart. I withdrew my sight from her.

When my coffee arrived, I asked the man if he knew the woman but he didn't. The man asked if I was a visitor because he had never seen me before. I introduced myself as a grocery store owner in his neighboring town and explained how I recently got to become one. He told me his name was Ruben and he lived in a small town just a few kilometers away. As Ruben had predicted, I loved the coffee very much. I don't think I need a new coffee maker anymore.

A few weeks ago, if you'd asked me to choose between driving a car and taking public transportation, there'd be no doubt my answer would have been the latter. But today I almost cried for joy when I saw the leased car arrive at the store. It may sound silly, but I felt like I was mobile again. People in this town normally walk or bike to get to places. Only occasionally would they use family cars for doing a lot of shopping or going to the coast. They don't, if ever, get out of town much.

After my shift was over, I took the car out for a spin. I drove to Amsterdam, had some jenever at *Wynand Fockink* and drove back. If my neighbors knew what I did, they might think I was mentally ill. It is bizarre – after living in another place for a long time, I forgot that I used to think like them.

Ever since I came back, I often wonder if I'm the one who is alienating people in town. Nah, could I? Johan told me he doesn't even chat with the customers who are actually friends of his parents'. He said it makes him feel like he lives in a big city. I told him he had the wrong idea about living in the city.

"I'm out of here as soon as I graduate from secondary school," Johan often announces.

He is just like me when I was his age. Eager to leave town, everything seems to suck here. Young people are moving out. I remember on my way to school, I used to see our retired old neighbors sitting by the windows inside their houses looking out. Though they treated us kids like their own grandchildren, the emotionless faces creeped me out. The town was, and still is, a stereotype of a small town. It seems like everybody knows everybody here. But even so, some people always prefer to keep to themselves. I noticed the awkwardness whenever a local greeted a non-local. It is funny if you think about it. Everyone was once an outsider somewhere, well, unless you never travel.

In the evening I stopped by Sokoke. I didn't expect it to be open at that hour, but luckily the lights were still on. Ruben was drying a coffee cup when I went in. I asked if all he does is dry coffee cups. He laughed at my silly joke. The coffee that Sokoke offers often has a wine-flavored taste, but tonight Ruben prepared one that embraces a citrus tone. He said it reminded him of his late wife. They used to drink it when they talked about visiting Kenya. Ruben's wife was killed in a ski accident many years ago. He then went to Nairobi to pursue the life they had both dreamed of. I had so many questions on my lips, but I really have just met the guy. When he offered me a second cup, I went back to the wine-flavored kind. Ruben took another citrus one. He talked about his three daughters. None of them are over twenty-five and all of them live abroad.

"Why do the young always want to leave town?" I complained. "I mean, it's not like other places guarantee a better life."

For a brief moment I forgot I was once so desperate to leave my town.

"That is why they always go back, one way or another." Ruben winked at me as a response to my grumbling.

I offered to help him clean up, but Ruben said his guests should only worry about drinking coffee. I thought about what Ruben said while driving home. Maybe he's right. Maybe sooner or later, one way or another, we all go back to where we came from. But what if we choose not to?

There was an ambulance parked outside the store early this afternoon. I didn't see what happened because I was in the office filling out tax papers and was on and off the phone with the accountant. To avoid distractions, I shut the office door to keep out the siren coming from the street. I have never been the type of person who pokes her nose around wherever there's an accident. Nevertheless I was interrupted by Hans' knock on the door. He told me that one of our regular customers had collapsed on the street after she walked out of the store. It was an old lady named Anne Vermeersch. People who know her call her Mrs. Brown.

I remember Mrs. Brown. I used to go to the same secondary school with her son Jonathan. He was in his last year when I entered my first. Mrs. Brown was always nice to us kids whenever she chaperoned school events. She was a kind and elegant person. Mrs. Brown's husband is an American. They met in the States when Mrs. Brown went to study there. She was the first girl in town who studied abroad. When Mrs. Brown's father got sick, they moved back to town. Mr. Brown's arrival caused quite a stir. But it wasn't in a negative way. People were more curious than concerned. Kids in school used to tease Jonathan for being a mix. Back then there weren't many mixed children in West Flanders. They would call him a *Yankee*. Jonathan was a quiet, mature boy. He never once confronted those who called him names. Mother said he was just like his father. I sometimes saw Mr. and Mrs. Brown shopping together in Aunt Hilde's store when I helped out in the summer. Mr. Brown was even quieter than Jonathan. I don't remember ever hearing him speak. It was always Mrs. Brown doing the talking. Mother tried a few times to invite the Browns over for dinner, but they never came. Mother gave up trying after the fourth time.

Jonathan was a model student in school. He did well in exams, he never caused trouble and whenever there was a competition, teachers always appointed him to represent the school. It's like he was perfect. But I remember I didn't like his face much. His chin was simply too long for my taste. Mother asked Jonathan to tutor me once, but he got annoyed in the middle of the session when I asked him to say something with an American accent. He got up and left. Mrs. Brown brought him back the next day to apologize for his rude behavior, but afterwards he never came back and I failed French that year. Since then, I have never really seen him again. I don't think he was avoiding me but if he was, he did a hell of a good job. I was just being a silly kid. He shouldn't hold a grudge against me for that. Or should he?

There was one summer I ran into Mr. Brown waiting for the bus alone. It was very unusual to see him outside by himself. He's a fully functioning grown man, I think, but somehow whenever I saw Mr. Brown, he was always accompanied by his wife. I wanted to turn around and walk away, but I had to catch that bus because I was already late for a meet-up with the girls in the neighboring town. Mr. Brown is an average-looking Caucasian man. If no one had told me, I wouldn't have guessed that he is not from around here. Though he does look like one of those typical professors you see in American movies. They often wear button-down shirts, with or without a tie, and blazers that have suede elbow pads. And that's what he was wearing when I ran into him that day. I don't know if Mr. Brown can speak West Flemish. I greeted him in English that day.

"Good morning, Mr. Brown," I said as I arrived at the bus stop.

"Good morning," Mr. Brown replied as he looked at me.

Then he looked away. I didn't have the courage to go on with the conversation. I also looked away. On the bus I chose a seat that was away from Mr. Brown. I think that is the only one-on-one interaction I have ever had with him.

At Mother's funeral, as I vaguely remember, the Browns were sitting discreetly at the back. The next year, I heard Jonathan left for the States. And a few years later, Aunt Hilde told me in a letter that Jonathan had married a girl there and decided to stay in the States. Mrs. Brown liked to talk about her son when they came shopping at the store. Aunt Hilde loved to hear stories of other people's children since she didn't have any.

Hans was the one who phoned the ambulance. He said he would visit Mrs. Brown after work and was wondering if I'd like to join him. I refused. I am not good when it comes to hospitals.

I was putting vegetables on the refrigerated shelf when Hans came and told me the unfortunate news. Mrs. Brown was pronounced dead yesterday soon after arriving at the hospital. Hans was there in the evening when they moved her to the morgue. The hospital gave Mr. Brown a plastic bag that Mrs. Brown had been carrying. Hans saw Mr. Brown open the bag and take out two blocks of cheese. Apparently that was the reason Mrs. Brown came back to the store for a second time that afternoon.

The last time I saw Mrs. Brown was at Mother's funeral. I don't think I actually talked to her at all. Perhaps I did. I don't remember much about that day. I hate funerals.

I could tell by Hans' red eyes that he'd been emotional. I didn't know he and Mrs. Brown were close. Hans said they weren't friends or anything, but whenever Mrs. Brown was in the store she always asked how he was. She was a really nice customer. The funeral is this Saturday and there'll be a service held at the Brown residence. I remember the house very well, not because I used to go there a lot but because it is located in a remote area. Yes, you can still find a remote area even in a town like this. Before the Browns, I don't recall ever seeing anyone living there. People guessed that Mr. Brown felt awkward living right next to the locals, which was why after Mrs. Brown's father died, they moved to a property like that.

I don't really know much about Mr. Brown. I think no one in this town does. Whatever bits and pieces we heard about him came from Mrs. Brown. We know his first name is Jeff. He was born and raised in the States, but I don't remember where exactly. Mr. and Mrs. Brown got married and lived in the States for a short time. They moved back here solely because of the medical condition of Mrs. Brown's father.

Another thing I remember is that I have never seen Mr. Brown having a conversation with anyone in town. He greets people and there have been some exchanges of words on rare occasions, but I've never seen Mr. Brown chatting. I used to think he was just a shy, quiet person like his son. But later I came to realize that Mr. Brown doesn't really speak the language. Maybe that's why Mrs. Brown was with him all the time. One evening when I was helping Mother for dinner, she told me that Mr. Brown was a writer.

"Why don't you go and talk to Mr. Brown, since you like

to write too," Mother suggested.

"No, thanks. I am not interested in writing about fast food and obesity." As a teenage girl at a rebellious age, I always responded in a mocking tone. To tell the truth, it was quite a thrill to know what Mr. Brown did for a living.

Soon I gave up on writing. I guess it was just a phase, like every ambition I have ever had in my life. I am normally not a quitter – well, at least I don't see myself as one. But somehow I always find myself switching from one path to another. I just can't seem to hold on to something after a time. I hope I have changed because I want to be, and I think I am, serious about this new job of mine.

Hans volunteered to help out with the funeral. He is going to notify people who knew Mrs. Brown and make the necessary arrangements.

I hate funerals.

I Googled Mr. Brown today. It came up with around 474,000,000 results. First one on the list was someone from Canada also named Jeff Brown who has multiple professions. Obviously, this was not Mr. Brown. I kept clicking on pages until I came across something on page seventeen. It was an article link from a local publisher based in Schnellville, Indiana, USA. Mother used to say that the name of the place where Mrs. Brown studied in the States reminded her of Indiana Jones. Now this one sounded more like a potential match. I clicked on the link and a PDF popped open in a new window. It was not an article. It was a collection of poems written by Jeff Brown, possibly our Mr. Brown. I spent the next two hours reading and rereading those poems. They were beautifully written. I was impressed. Since I was not sure if this was Mr. Brown, I decided to write the publisher an e-mail in hopes of learning about the author. I felt like a stalker.

It was rainy and windy the whole day today. It seems like the winter I knew has finally returned. Though Fridays often get quite busy in the store, I gave Hans a day off today since he is helping Mr. Brown with the funeral.

"It's going to be a nice funeral," Hans said. I never understand why people describe a funeral as nice. I think I can agree that a funeral is well organized, but nice would never be the word I'd choose. Or perhaps when people use the word nice they are referring to the decoration or its formality. Either way, I still hate funerals.

Sokoke is closed today because Ruben is spending the weekend with his sister's family in Brussels. If I didn't know Ruben personally, I would label him an irresponsible café owner. With my newfound paradise being unavailable, I decided to go out for a jog. It's got to be more than twenty years since I jogged in town. Each time before my jog, I would study a map of the town that I had for years and draw a shape of some creature by connecting the streets with a pen. The town is not big, but I somehow could always come up with a new shape. I was quite proud of my imagination. Now I wonder if my old stuff is still in Aunt Hilde's attic. I'm sure my map is still lying up there somewhere.

My time in this town was okay. It wasn't like I hated it or anything. Life was actually quite easy. But I always felt I didn't belong. Jogging was the most effective method of escaping the town without physically moving out of it. My map of this town must be completely different than those of the locals. I used to think my imagination would satisfy my adventurous nature, and that was that, but of course it didn't.

People who jog know that in order to be a good jogger, you should always keep a steady pace. Inhale through the nose and exhale through the mouth. And the best breathing rhythm is two inhalations followed by two exhalations. When you follow the rules you can jog long and purposefully. I could never stick to this nonsense. I found it difficult to keep track of how many times I inhaled and exhaled. I always got confused and ended up being quickly out of breath. I did what was best for me: one inhalation followed by one exhalation.

Normally you don't see people walking around in the streets after dark here, so I always jog at night to avoid unplanned social encounters. There would be nights that the streets weren't expectedly vacated. Sometimes Mr. Verhaest would be walking his dog, or Mrs. Derijcke would be cleaning her front windows. When those moments occurred, I couldn't be gladder that I had my best friend in my pocket, a Sony Walkman. The Rolling Stones cassette I borrowed from Father never saw the light of day after I began jogging. I came across their 1980 album *Emotional Rescue* in Father's collection when I was looking for something, anything, to listen to. Father used to play the number She's so Cold in the car when he was happy. I hardly listened to that song anymore after Mother died.

Though each time I preferred to jog on a different route, there was one location that I returned to again and again. It was a factory that collected used or destroyed bulbs and fluorescent tubes. The broken ones gave an incredible silver glow at night. It looked like an alien landing site. I often took breaks there by the gate. The gate tonight was not locked and the factory seemed to have been abandoned and vacant for years. Without thinking, I barged in.

The moonlight struggled behind the clouds. It was not the brightest night. I cautiously followed the driveway and arrived at the front door of the main building. On the door there was a sign that said KEEP OUT. The sign looked recent. It convinced me not to go in. I walked ahead alongside the building and saw a faint glow peaking out of the dark behind the far end of the building. For no reason, I came to a halt. There were only a few meters between the mysterious glow and me, but my brain was telling my feet not to move any further. The air was dead still.

As I was wondering why I couldn't bring myself to investigate, a squirrel jumped out of the bush for my attention. I looked away for a second. When I turned back, the glow was gone. It was dark again.

On my way to the Brown residence, I saw two concrete staircases lying on their sides in the front yard of Mr. Van Rykeghem's house. They looked newly made and both of them weren't painted. To be perfectly honest, I don't think I've ever seen staircases prior to their completed installation. They seemed much larger on their own. The natural grey color and how they were positioned somehow constructed a sculptural atmosphere. Mr. Van Rykeghem's front yard was thus transformed into an open-air art space like the *Middelheimmuseum* in *Antwerpen*. But on a day like today, the two stone, cold, tomblike staircases reminded me even more that there was a funeral going on just a few blocks away. Have I mentioned that I hate funerals?

I didn't think my stomach could handle the actual burial and all, so I skipped the main funeral and went straight for the reception at the Brown residence. The living room was arranged in a peculiar fashion. The room was divided in half. On one side stood only tables and the other only chairs. There were food and drinks on the tables, and the chairs outnumbered the guests. When I arrived, I saw Jonathan walking in and out of the room greeting the guests. I wasn't aware that he was back in town. But of course he came back; it was his mother's funeral. We ran into each other in the hallway, and he introduced me to his wife, Rebecca, and their eight-year-old son, Jimmy. We had a brief chat before they moved on to the rest of the guests. I couldn't help but notice that Jonathan seemed to have changed. He was not the shy boy I once knew. Rebecca looked like a fine lady, properly dressed, but you could tell she was not at all comfortable being in a new environment where everyone speaks a language she doesn't know. She told me that this was the first time she'd met Mr. Brown and it was a shame that she never got to know Mrs. Brown better. Except for the standard greetings, Jimmy didn't say anything else to me during my conversation with his parents. He was as shy as his father back in the old days. When Jonathan was away to get more refreshments, Rebecca and Jimmy isolated themselves in a corner. They, including Jonathan, hardly spoke to Mr. Brown. It seemed to me that Jonathan had come back to town for Mrs. Brown and Mrs. Brown only, and Rebecca and Jimmy had come because of Jonathan. Towards the end of the reception, in his southern accent, Mr. Brown managed to compose a few sentences to thank the guests.

"Thank you all for coming," Mr. Brown said. "My wife lived a full life, but I sure will miss her."

Hearing this brought tears to my eyes. I guess it reminded me of Father when Mother died. I went into the bathroom to try to calm myself down. When I came out of the bathroom, I realized the guests were gone. I collected my coat and purse and went to say goodbye to the family and give them my condolences one last time. As I was about to exit through the living room, I saw Jonathan and Mr. Brown sitting on the chairs in the hallway. I had a feeling they were discussing something serious, so I slipped back into the living room. I didn't mean to eavesdrop, but I couldn't help overhearing their conversation.

"I thought Mother said you quit smoking," Jonathan said.

"When have I ever been a quitter?"

"Very funny, Father," Jonathan said. "Anyway, mind if I bum one?"

I heard a few snicks when they tried to make the lighter work. The conversation continued.

"So what happens next?" Jonathan asked.

"What do you mean by what happens next?" Mr. Brown replied.

"I want to make a suggestion," Jonathan offered. "I think you should come and live with us in the States."

"Why do you think that?" Mr. Brown asked.

"Come on, Father, you know better than I do. You came here because Mom needed to take care of Grandpa. But now both of them are gone, so you don't have to stay here anymore," Jonathan elaborated. "It's not like you are so integrated or anything. I mean, you don't even talk to people here. When was the last time you had a chat with any of them?"

"And that's your answer to everything? When you feel you don't belong, you just leave?" Mr. Brown questioned. "You have no right to talk to me about where I should feel at home."

"At least I speak the language. I'm more a local here than you are," Jonathan said.

"If that's how you feel then why did you leave?" Mr. Brown asked.

The silence continued for a moment.

"Anyway, thanks for the offer." Mr. Brown made his conclusion, "I'm staying."

I left through the backdoor in the kitchen before either one of them could catch me listening.

There was an incident in the store today. Mr. Brown sort of broke down after a short encounter with our new cashier, Mrs. Vereecke. Mrs. Vereecke had been a devoted housewife and a wonderful mother for over three decades. Now with her children all married and her husband spending most of his time in the garden, Mrs. Vereecke thought she should find something to do too. Something that would make her feel useful. I like Mrs. Vereecke. Her use of words reminds me of Mother.

I was in the back doing inventory when the incident occurred. Mrs. Vereecke explained to me what happened. Around noon Mr. Brown came into the store. It was his first visit after Mrs. Brown's passing, and more importantly it was his first time alone in the store. Mrs. Vereecke said that Mr. Brown already seemed nervous when he arrived at the check-out counter. She was concerned about Mr. Brown's body language, yet Mrs. Vereecke tried being normal with him. She actually thought Mr. Brown was some kind of mentally-challenged person. Mrs. Vereecke said when Mr. Brown's bank-card didn't work in the machine, she asked if he had another one on him. Mr. Brown did not respond and began to pack his purchases into his shopping bag. Mrs. Vereecke then asked for a second time. She said Mr. Brown just looked extremely agitated and didn't seem to be paying attention. That's when Mrs. Vereecke was convinced that Mr. Brown might have either mental or physical disabilities. She then decided to reach over and take the wallet out of Mr. Brown's hands. It might not have been the smartest thing to do, but she thought she was helping him. At that exact moment, Mr. Brown became hysterical. Mrs. Vereecke said Mr. Brown was shouting and trying to grab his wallet, but he pulled too hard and the wallet slipped out of his hand and landed on the ground. There were a few coins that fell out of the wallet and spilled all over the floor. Mr. Brown got down on his knees and tried to scoop up the coins with his hands. Mrs. Vereecke felt bad about what happened so she also got down, trying to help Mr. Brown. And that's when Mr. Brown had a breakdown and pushed her. Mrs. Vereecke hit her head on the side of the counter. She then got up and called the police. It happened so fast that even Hans, who was only a few meters away stacking cleaning products, couldn't assist Mr. Brown in time and stop the whole thing from happening. When the police arrived, Mr. Brown was still sitting on the ground holding his wallet. I saw this as I came to the front. Without knowing what had happened, I insisted to the police that it must be a misunderstanding. Mrs. Vereecke didn't press charges. The police then escorted Mr. Brown out of the store. We were all in shock. I called Mrs. Vereecke into my office for the details.

"When you asked him for a second card," I asked out of concern, "did you say it in English?"

"No," Mrs. Vereecke seemed puzzled. "Why?"

I then explained to Mrs. Vereecke the story of Mr. Brown.

Mr. Brown must be overwhelmed by all the changes in his life. From now on he would live a life without a personal translator and communicator. I thought Mr. Brown understood our language. Perhaps he got stressed because he was trying to say something to Mrs. Vereecke but couldn't. Mrs. Vereecke said she couldn't speak English and asked what she should do when Mr. Brown was in the store next time. I told her to come get Hans or me when that happened.

The image of Mr. Brown sitting on the ground holding his wallet in his hands stuck in my mind the whole afternoon. He looked embarrassed and powerless.

Before she went back to work, Mrs. Vereecke brought me the two bags of groceries that Mr. Brown had purchased. He forgot them. I decided to take a short break and bring them to Mr. Brown. I took a peek inside the bags. There was no cheese.

Mr. Brown opened the door after I knocked three times, and I told him who I was and why I was there. He had a woman's cardigan in his hand. I figured he might be packing Mrs. Brown's things. I gave him the groceries.

"Is Jonathan back in the States?" I asked.

"No, not yet," Mr. Brown responded while looking at the cardigan in his hand. "They are staying for a few more days."

"How nice," I said. "Are they staying here?"

Mr. Brown seemed preoccupied.

"Mr. Brown?" I said.

"Yes, no, no," Mr. Brown answered. "They are staying in a hotel."

I suddenly felt I should go.

"I should go, Mr. Brown," I said. "Take care."

"Thank you, uh..." Mr. Brown sounded as if he hadn't finished his sentence.

"Marie," I said. "Marie Vandenberghe." I think Mr. Brown knows my name, but I thought I would take this chance to reintroduce myself. As I drove away from Mr. Brown's house, I saw Jonathan walking down the street from the opposite direction.

Since two weeks ago, the store has had a new customer. We now deliver fresh vegetables and pastries to a local community school in a neighboring town. The school provides Dutch (Flemish) courses to people of all ages. The language courses are certified and funded by the province. According to Principal Seynaeve, a fifty-two-year-old man who was born and raised in *Dentergem,* there are more and more immigrants residing in West Flanders. The school wants to support and help these new residents to integrate into the local community, and the first step is learning the language.

I remember the day I first met Principal Seynaeve. It was in his office, and we had a meeting about our future partnership. The school is a small institution with limited staff so he practically does everything. It was a small office, no bigger than mine in the store, and there were three ferns standing in a corner. They were lined up by size. The walls were white and it made the ferns look really green. Before we started, Principal Seynaeve offered me a cup of tea accompanied with a *beuterkoek*. I told him my aunt used to bring me those on Sundays. He said he was never a fan of them, but one summer a girl taught him to like them.

"Her name wouldn't be Hilde Maes, would it?" I asked with an excited tone. Principal Seynaeve wondered if that was the name of my aunt. I said yes. He said it was a lovely name, but no, the girl's name was not Hilde Maes. After we came to an agreement about the deliveries, Principal Seynaeve showed me around the school. There were six classrooms in the building, two big ones and four small ones. Each of them had a giant window in one wall. He said the demand for Dutch courses was increasing so they were thinking of moving to another premises, but it probably wouldn't happen until 2016. On the second floor was their cafeteria, and it was packed with students and staff when Principal Seynaeve guided me there. Most of them were non-Caucasians.

When Principal Seynaeve was away to get us some coffee, a Moroccan man walked towards our table with a tray in his hands. He looked quite young with his leather jacket and the styling gel meticulously applied to his hair. As he arrived at the table, he spoke properly and politely, with a West Flemish accent.

"Is this seat free?" he asked.

"Yes, it is," I answered.

He smiled and sat down. His perfect accent made me curious about him.

"Was it a hard language for you to learn as an adult?" I asked, with admiration in my tone. "Your West Flemish accent is impressive."

"I was born and grew up in *Roeselare*," he said with a smile, "so I've had twenty-six years of practice. That helped."

I dropped my head in embarrassment. I think my neck went from white to red in seconds. What was I thinking? It's 2013, for heaven's sake. And to think I had lived in *Antwerpen* for years. I should know better.

"Oh, my God," I responded with my apple-red face. "I am so sorry, I wasn't thinking straight."

"Don't worry about it," he said. "It's an honest mistake, you know. You're in a language school for immigrants and you see a foreign-looking person."

"No, please allow me to apologize," I explained. "I shouldn't have assumed you're not a local."

"Like I said," he winked at me as he continued, "don't worry about it."

Before I thought of the next thing to say, Principal Seynaeve came back and sat down with two cups of coffee.

"I see you've met Rachid, one of our best teachers," Principal Seynaeve announced to me as he put sugar in his coffee.

Not only was Rachid not a foreigner who came to learn Dutch, he was actually a model teacher teaching the language. All of a sudden I thought of what Grandpa Andre once asked Josephine, *Hasn't anyone ever told you not to judge a book by its cover?* If I'd had a horse with me, I would've ridden off already. Rachid didn't mention my little unintentional blunder during our conversation with Principal Seynaeve. For that I was grateful.

On my way out of the building, I picked up a few brochures from the reception. I thought I might put them in the store.

Jonathan came to the store today and asked to see me. Mr. Brown told him that I'd brought his groceries the other day. Jonathan wanted to thank me in person, and also he needed someone to talk to about his father. He said it might sound crazy, but I was the only person in town he felt comfortable with. I didn't think it was crazy, but I admit it did come as a surprise to me. I asked him if he knew about his father's breakdown in the store. Jonathan said that yes, the police contacted him at the hotel and told him what had happened. He also apologized on behalf of Mr. Brown. I was in the middle of work when Jonathan visited, so I gave him the address of Sokoke and told him we could meet and talk there tonight around eight.

"Oudenburg?" Jonathan asked skeptically.

"The coffee is good," I assured him. "See you tonight."

It was a quarter to nine when Jonathan finally arrived at Sokoke. He said Jimmy wouldn't sleep unless he read him bedtime stories. I wasn't upset with Jonathan for being late. If anything, it was nice to hear he cared about his son so much. I recommended the coffee with the wine flavor to Jonathan, but he ordered the citrus one instead. Now I wonder, maybe men prefer citrus? We watched Ruben as he prepared the coffee. Neither of us spoke a word. I observed Jonathan's face while he observed Ruben. Jonathan definitely looked good for a forty-four-year-old. There were wrinkles here and there, but they just added more character. For the record, I don't fancy Jonathan. I was merely stunned by how much a person could change over the years. Seemed like the old Jonathan had vanished. Or perhaps, it was still the old him, only with new packaging.

"Damn," Jonathan praised, "that is some good coffee. Where did you find it?"

"Kenya," I answered at once. "Ruben is an expert on African coffee."

"Very nice," Jonathan said as he looked around the café. "But, no offense, you're making money here?"

Jonathan had a point. Every time I'm here, I hardly see other customers. I was curious to know Ruben's answer.

"Well," Ruben cleared his throat, "no."

"But," I said, not wanting to pry, "Hans said you've been open for a year now. How do you, uh…"

"Survive?" Jonathan took the word out of my mouth, and he wasn't afraid of prying. "Have you got other jobs or something?"

"I guess you'll never know," Ruben said as he took away our coffee cups. "More coffee?"

After our second round was served, Ruben excused himself and slipped into the back room. Jonathan took a sip of his coffee and then began to disclose what had been troubling him since he came back to town.

"I asked my father to come and live with us in the States," Jonathan said.

"You did? That's very nice of you," I said.

"But my father wants to stay."

"Did he say why he wants to stay?" I asked.

"No," Jonathan sighed. "But I think he's somehow convinced that he belongs here."

"And you don't think so?" I asked.

"How can he feel he belongs here?" Jonathan raised his voice a bit. "He doesn't even talk to people in town!"

"You may be right." I told him what I thought, "But is that the only way of measuring whether people belong or not?"

"He's always like that," Jonathan complained, "isolating himself from others."

"I heard he moved here just so Mrs. Brown could take care of her sick father," I said. "You've got to give him credit for that."

Jonathan fell into silence for a moment. "You know," Jonathan took another sip of his coffee, "the day before he had the meltdown, my father discovered a box full of VHS tapes labeled by year hidden in my mother's walk-in closet. I went to the house and we watched one."

"And?" I was curious.

"Apparently," Jonathan explained, "ever since they moved back here, every year on her birthday, my mother would record a short video to serve as a will in case something happened to her. And in the one that I saw, my mother talked about a wish."

"What kind of wish?" I asked, trying not to sound too excited.

"She wished that my father would overcome whatever obstacles he thinks he has and learn to speak the language."

Jonathan's eyes were watering. "She said she wouldn't be here for him forever, and when she was gone, she hoped my father wouldn't have to live a lonely life."

Jonathan said that in the video, Mrs. Brown made sure she was smiling when she told the wish. When Jonathan confronted Mr. Brown by asking him what he was going to do about Mrs. Brown's wish, Mr. Brown told Jonathan to leave and then stormed out of the room.

Ruben said he was closing down the place for the night soon, but if we wished, he would give us the key and we could stay longer. I thanked him and suggested he give the key to Jonathan because I should go too; tomorrow was another early day for me. Before I walked out of Sokoke, I asked Jonathan to stop by the store this week; I wanted to give him the brochure from Principal Seynaeve's school.

Today was the 10th 'Bakken met Sarah' at the store. It's an annual event that Sarah came up with to promote the bakery and connect with the local community. The event is family friendly, so we were expecting a lot of kids. For the past ten years on every first Sunday of March, Sarah has organized a baking contest where the old and new customers can come with their children to shape their own dough and compete for a prize. The contest is open to children under the age of twelve. According to Hans, it's a very popular event. Some families really look forward to it.

I had no clue there were so many things to take care of beforehand. For example, we needed to prepare a fair amount of dough so when the contest starts the children can just go right ahead and form it. I kneaded so much dough my arms were dead sore afterwards.

Jonathan came alone when I was covered in flour. I gave him the brochure of the language school. Before he left, Jonathan told me Rebecca might bring Jimmy here for the event. I was glad to hear that. After walking Jonathan out of the store, I dove back into the mountain of dough.

The event opened at 2 p.m. with Sarah's inspirational speech followed by another speech from a local politician. I wasn't so keen on the idea of involving a politician, but Sarah had her reasons. Soon the speeches were done, and the event kicked off. Hans was not kidding. People were crazy about this event. You heard children shouting and parents screaming. People who complain about the low birth rate should really witness this event. The whole thing went on for three hours. There were times I thought I might go deaf. Rebecca and Jimmy came after the official starting time of the contest, but I managed to save Jimmy one small piece of dough so he could participate. While Jimmy was traveling in his creative universe, Rebecca and I sat down and talked.

"I hope it's okay we came," Rebecca apologized. "Jonathan told me about the event and thought it could be fun for Jimmy."

"Of course," I assured Rebecca, "I am really happy you came." I poured Rebecca a cup of tea. "What have you been doing this past week? I haven't seen you since."

"I took Jimmy to visit some other places," Rebecca said. "It's our first time in Belgium, and Jonathan didn't want us to miss out on anything."

"Oh? I see," I said.

"For the record, I was against it. I wanted Jimmy to spend some time with his grandfather." Rebecca took a sip of her tea. "You know, this is the first time Jimmy has met him."

"Has Jimmy talked to Mr. Brown at the house?" I asked.

"Hardly," Rebecca said and sighed. "Jonathan hasn't let him."

"Why not?" I asked.

"I don't know. Maybe because Jonathan doesn't think his father was a good father." Rebecca seemed to feel awkward as she finished her sentence. "I'm sorry, I shouldn't be telling you this."

"It's okay," I said.

Rebecca then changed the subject. "I heard you're trying to help Jonathan's father learn your language?"

"Our new customer is a language school," I answered. "Most of the students are immigrants. After I heard about the tapes Mrs. Brown made, I thought perhaps it could help Mr. Brown."

"I hope so," Rebecca said. "I can't imagine living in a place and not being able to talk to people."

"You do know Mr. Brown already has some basic knowledge of the language, right?" I explained. "Just for some reason he has difficulties speaking it."

"That's strange," Rebecca said.

Sarah stood next to the oven and announced it was time to present the winners. All contestants looked excited while waiting for the results. The first and second prize went to two girls living just a few blocks away, and the third prize went to a boy from a neighboring town. Jimmy didn't win anything, but he told Rebecca he'd had fun. Jimmy showed me what he'd made, but I couldn't tell what it was.

"What is it?" I asked.

"It's a nose," Jimmy said. "Grandpa Jeff's nose."

"Oh?" I was puzzled. "Why Grandpa Jeff's nose?"

"Daddy said," Jimmy explained, "Grandma Anne used to kiss his nose three times when he was sad." Jimmy brought the bread-nose to his lips. "Grandpa Jeff looked sad. I thought maybe I could kiss it better."

Principal Seynaeve was in his office having a meeting with the teachers when I dropped off the delivery. I guess Rachid was in the meeting too. I like going to Principal Seynaeve's school. The racial mixture of students reminds me of *Antwerpen.*

I stood for a while by the railing along the gallery on the second floor, looking down at the little entrance square. The morning classes begin at 9 a.m. Most of the students who come to morning classes are older. I'm not surprised. It's quite logical. I saw a few small groups of elderly people chatting on the square. The big clock on the building showed it was a quarter to nine. I guess they were trying to catch up before class.

My attention soon went to a man who was standing alone in between the groups. He was not talking to anybody. With his back facing me I couldn't see his face, but when I saw the suede elbow pads on his blazer I thought it could be Mr. Brown. The man didn't move a hair. He was just standing there. Paralyzed. As I didn't feel like shouting across the square, I decided to go down and see if I was right. But when I got to the square, the man was gone. I looked around, but found no men wearing blazers with suede elbow pads. I stood there as my mind wandered, and before I knew it I was alone on the square.

Today I decided to be an unexpected guest. I went to visit Mr. Brown. I took some groceries with me. Mr. Brown was skeptical about my visit, but I was prepared.

"I brought cheesecake," I said.

"Don't you know that old people shouldn't eat too much cheese?" Mr. Brown responded as he turned and walked back into the house without closing the door. I followed him in. It was easier than I'd expected, to be honest. I thought he would slam the door in my face or something. Instead, Mr. Brown guided me into the kitchen.

"Tea?" Mr. Brown asked.

"Yes, please," I said. "Thank you."

I wasn't asked if I wanted sugar or milk, but Mr. Brown prepared the tea with a certain precision and manner that reminded me of those properly trained butlers in some period drama you see on television. There was a door next to the window behind the dining table. It opened to a little path at the back of the house and I thought it led to the church. I was sitting at a low table when Mr. Brown brought us two slices of cheesecake plated on separate china. I complimented him on the table while Mr. Brown went to fetch the utensils. He sat down and thanked me for the cake. Mr. Brown said that since Mrs. Brown's passing he hasn't had any cheesecake. He cut a small piece off his slice with a fork and put it in his mouth. Mr. Brown took his time tasting what he'd been missing. He then poured more tea in both of our cups.

"So, Marie," Mr. Brown asked, "why are you here?"

"Do you know," I said, "that Jonathan has been talking about you to me?"

"What about me?" Mr. Brown asked.

"He," I hesitated a bit, "he is worried about you."

"There is nothing to worry about," Mr. Brown stated.

"Jonathan seems to think otherwise."

Mr. Brown didn't respond to my last sentence and turned his attention back to the plate. I waited as I watched him finish his cake.

"He also told me about the tapes," I continued. "The tapes that Mrs. Brown made."

Mr. Brown seemed surprised that Jonathan had told me about the tapes. "What did he say?" I could tell by his voice that Mr. Brown was not comfortable with me knowing.

"He said," I answered, "Mrs. Brown was worried about you being lonely when she'd be gone."

Mr. Brown didn't respond. He stood up and walked to the kitchen counter. He returned the rest of the cake to its box and put it in the fridge. I suddenly had an urge to say what came to mind.

"Don't push people away, Mr. Brown," I said.

"I let you in, didn't I?"

Mr. Brown moved on to clean the utensils in the sink. I got up and offered to help, but he refused. I stood in front of the window by the backdoor. I looked in the direction of the church.

"I think there's a communion going on this morning. Would you like to go and see it?" I suggested.

"No, thanks," Mr. Brown answered. "I didn't even enjoy Jonathan's communion."

"I think I'll take a look," I said. "See you next time, Mr. Brown."

"I went to that school you recommended to Jonathan," Mr. Brown announced when I pushed the backdoor open. I stepped back and let the door close.

"What did you think about the school?" I asked.

"A joke."

"A joke?" I asked incredulously. "What made you think that?"

"Did you know they have a Moroccan teacher there?" Mr. Brown complained.

"Yes, and I think he is well qualified," I said confidently.

"Teaching Flemish?" Mr. Brown questioned suspiciously.

"He was born and raised here," I explained. "He *is* a West Flemish man."

"Anyway," Mr. Brown concluded, "he's not from this town. I prefer someone local."

"Why is that?" I asked.

"Anne was from here," Mr. Brown answered.

On my way to the church, I couldn't stop thinking about the conversation. I heard once on the radio that most Americans are conservative. I wondered if that was the case with Mr. Brown. Later that evening, I thought about the conversation again while I jogged.

At 4 a.m. this morning I woke up from a nightmare. I haven't had nightmares since I was in school. I dreamt I was in between two cliffs trying to get from one cliff to the other, on a fine rope made of paper. When I was nearly halfway across, a group of seagulls flew by me, and I lost my balance and fell into the mouth of a giant lizard. I didn't fall back asleep after that.

During lunch break, I went to the bookstore in the center looking for books that depict dreams. I have never been a superstitious person, but because it's been years since I've had such a ghastly and nasty nightmare, I thought seeking a little explanation wouldn't hurt. There were so many choices on the shelf that I decided to go for the obvious, Sigmund Freud. After I was back in my office, Hans told me Mr. Brown had been in the store while I was out.

"Nothing happened, I hope," I said.

"No," Hans said, "but he was looking for you."

Sarah told me she had the same book when she saw mine on the desk. She found certain theories of Freud's interesting, but for some reason she'd never finished reading the book. Something about the line spacing – Sarah said the lines were too close to each other. She was thinking of retyping the whole book with her own spacing.

Jonathan called in the afternoon. He wanted to invite me over for dinner this Saturday with the family. It'd be at his father's house and Rebecca was going to cook. The store normally closes at six, so I told him I could be there around eight. I guess I would find out then what Mr. Brown wanted from me this afternoon.

By the end of the day, I was convinced that today was one of those days when you feel like you're so close to finishing a puzzle but you're missing the last piece. It tests your ingenuity and patience. With this incompleteness hanging over my head, I went out jogging. The town was dead quiet. There was no sign of Mr. Verhaest walking his dog or Mrs. Derijcke washing her windows. Even the full moon tonight seemed a bit apprehensive. I tried to ignore all the funny episodes that took place today and concentrate on my breathing, thinking *it's just one of those days.* The odd atmosphere of tonight reminded me of the night I jogged crying. During my last two years in secondary school, I often slept over at Aunt Hilde's.

It's probably not very nice of me to say, but when I was that age I sometimes wished Aunt Hilde was my mother.

On one particular evening, Aunt Hilde asked me to clean up my room because I had promised her. It was a Friday night and I was planning to have a lazy evening to salvage what was left of me from the mentally exhausting day at school. But Aunt Hilde pointed out that a promise is a promise. I don't remember exactly what had gotten into me, but somehow I started arguing, and all of a sudden the word *zot wuf* slipped out of my mouth. I then ran out of the house. I ran and I cried. It wasn't because of the argument I cried. It wasn't because Aunt Hilde insisted that I clean my room I cried. I cried because I realized, for the first time, how cruel I could be. I loved Aunt Hilde so much it hurt. Later that evening when I got back to Aunt Hilde's, she was waiting for me in my room. I cried again. Aunt Hilde didn't yell at me or scold me for being disrespectful. Instead she comforted me.

"Why are you crying?" Aunt Hilde teased me. "I should be the one that's crying."

It was only years later I truly understood why I cried that night. Although I never apologized to Aunt Hilde with words, I know she had figured out that my tears were my apology. A year later, when Father died, Aunt Hilde told me I could move in with her and that she would take care of me. She said I was practically already living in her house anyway, but I had decided to leave town. Aunt Hilde offered to take me to the train station; she wanted a proper goodbye. I was never good at goodbyes, so I told her there was no need. I could take the bus.

I wasn't sure if it was the moonlight that night or the pollen in the air, but Aunt Hilde's eyes were shimmering like a crystal chandelier. Before I came downstairs, I carved *Keep my room clean for me* on the wall next to my nightstand. I gave Aunt Hilde a big hug and off I went. It was the last time I saw Aunt Hilde. People often questioned why and thought how crazy it was that in all those years, I never went back to my hometown when it was just a two-hour train ride away. I used to shrug and make up all possible excuses, but the truth is I didn't think I could ever find the right answer. When I moved back a few weeks ago, my room was clean like I'd asked. Aunt Hilde must have thought I'd come back one day. But I didn't.

Standing in front of my words on the wall, I hope Aunt Hilde saw my apology tonight.

We were lined up shoulder to shoulder in the hallway between the living room and the dining room waiting for Rebecca to recite tonight's menu. She shyly announced that she would be serving food from her home state, New Jersey. I've heard of New Jersey. They are famous for their bedroom communities and various types of hot dogs. *Are we having hot dogs tonight?* I wondered.

"I don't know if Marie knows," Rebecca said, "but New Jersey is a state of many cultures, including Italian and Cuban. So tonight I am serving you *tomato pie* and *Moros y Cristianos.*"

The food looked good. I have never had Cuban food before, so I was quite thrilled. The long dining table was properly set and we were seated like this:

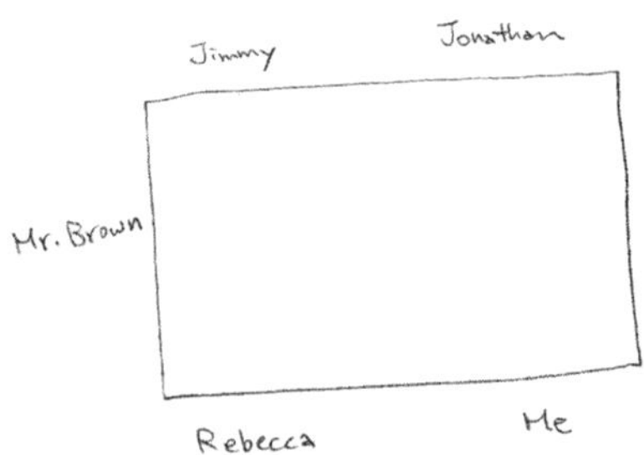

Mr. Brown was rearranging his utensils when I thought of his visit to the store the other day.

"Hans told me you were looking for me when I was out to lunch the other day," I said to Mr. Brown. "What was it you wanted to see me for?"

"You were at the store?" Jonathan asked before Mr. Brown could answer my question.

"Yes," Mr. Brown said, "but it doesn't matter now."

Rebecca sat down after she made sure everyone had enough food on their plates. Jimmy negotiated with Jonathan to trade his black beans for half of Jonathan's tomato pie. Jonathan said no, but then Mr. Brown cut his tomato pie in two and put one half on Jimmy's plate.

"Please don't do that," Jonathan said.

Mr. Brown brought the half tomato pie back to his plate and took a sip of wine. We ate quietly. I tried to break the ice by asking if Jimmy understood Flemish or, even, West Flemish. Rebecca said Jonathan had tried to teach Jimmy, but it wasn't an adequate learning environment back home. Even though Jimmy tried, he could only say a few basic words. Jonathan made a remark implying that unlike Mr. Brown, at least Jimmy was willing to try.

"Don't start," Rebecca said to Jonathan. "We have a guest."

"It's okay," Jonathan said. "Marie knows about Father."

Mr. Brown didn't appear to be offended. Perhaps he was now used to Jonathan's sarcasm. Or do I dare say, anger.

"But it's all going to be fine soon," Jonathan said while holding a wine glass in his hand. "Right, Father?"

Mr. Brown sat there unresponsive, and wordless. I didn't wish to pry, but clearly Jonathan wanted Mr. Brown to say something. I became really curious.

"What's going on?" I asked.

"My father is coming back to the States with us," Jonathan said.

"Really?" I said. "I thought Mr. Brown wanted to stay," I looked over at Mr. Brown. "When did you decide?"

Without responding to my question, Mr. Brown got up and walked out of the dining room. Jonathan put down his wine glass and excused himself. The evening was getting awkward. I felt like I should just go, but there were still two-thirds of my Moros y Cristianos left and I hadn't even touched the tomato pie. To leave now would be very inconsiderate.

"It's just us girls then," Rebecca said while pouring me and herself another glass of wine. When she leaned forward, one side of her long blonde wavy hair fell to the front and covered half of her face. Rebecca quickly tucked it back behind her ear. "Cheers," she said.

For a woman in her mid-forties, Rebecca looked young. Her features and her slim figure reminded me of Annick Christiaens in the movie *Wildschut.* I didn't tell Rebecca. I've learned not everyone likes to be told that they look like somebody else. As we continued the meal without the men, Jimmy asked if he could go and watch cartoons while he ate.

"Okay, but just this once," Rebecca said. She ruffled his

hair with her fingers before Jimmy ran off. For a moment, I wondered if Jimmy wanted to use the TV to drown out the arguing coming from upstairs. Guess I wasn't the only one who was aware of the muffled argument that had started a while ago.

After Rebecca poured us a third glass of wine, she started to talk about her and Jonathan. They met in New York while they were both doing internships at the same computer company. This August they would be twenty years together and ten years married, and in all those years Jonathan had hardly talked about Mr. and Mrs. Brown. Well, he talked about Mrs. Brown but not Mr. Brown. Rebecca said four months after Jimmy was born, Mrs. Brown flew to New York and stayed with them for five days. Rebecca remembered how happy Mrs. Brown was when she held Jimmy in her arms and how she soothed crying Jimmy by giving him three kisses on his nose. At the funeral, it comforted Rebecca greatly to know that Mrs. Brown had got to hold Jimmy once.

She asked if I had ever been to the States. I said no. I think The Netherlands is pretty much the only foreign country I have ever been to – well, except the time in *Watou* with Father when I was little. There was this crossroad that functioned as the border separating Belgium and France. I saw a sign marked *Belgium* on one side of the road and a few meters away another marked *France*. The fact that the distance between two countries was only the width of a street fascinated me. We got out of the car and walked down the road in the direction of France. For fifteen minutes, I was in France.

"And London?" Rebecca asked while pouring us another glass of wine.

I don't remember if I answered Rebecca, but her question made me think of Aunt Hilde and her personal history with London. When Grandpa Andre hosted those black-tie events, often there would be a few English clients coming from London. They always brought the fanciest British tea with them. Aunt Hilde was crazy about those teas.

One day Grandpa Andre decided to take Aunt Hilde with him on a business trip to London. Aunt Hilde couldn't sleep the night before and spent hours packing. On the departing afternoon, she was waiting in her room in the wool dress that Josephine had made for her. She waited and waited. Aunt

Hilde didn't get to go to London that day. It was only hours later she was told that Grandpa Andre and Grandma Katrien had died in a fatal car crash. Aunt Hilde allowed herself to be discouraged and never mentioned London again.

* *

I must have drifted off after that fourth glass of wine. There was a blanket covering me when I got up from the sofa. I don't even remember how I ended up on the sofa, in the living room. The TV was off and the house was very quiet. *Where is everybody?* I thought. The clock on the wall showed it was five minutes to midnight. I waited for my head to wake up before I got up and looked for my coat. When I walked into the hallway, I noticed that the door from the room next to the living room was slightly open. I gently pushed it open wider and saw an armchair, with its back facing me, and a TV that was playing what seemed to be one of the tapes Mrs. Brown had recorded. I stayed and watched.

In the video, Mrs. Brown was standing in front of a white wall in a blue pantsuit. Her hair was tied up in a neat ponytail. She began by saying how much she loved Jonathan and Mr. Brown, and then moved on to explain where she kept all the important documents and how Mr. Brown should handle the finances when she was gone. She also showed and praised the birthday presents she got from Mr. Brown and Jonathan. The picture went black for a second and when it came back, Mrs. Brown told her wish.

The TV was turned off before Mrs. Brown finished talking, and a man got up from the chair and switched on the light. It was Mr. Brown. I stepped inside the room when he retrieved the tape from the machine.

"I know about Mrs. Brown's wish," I said.

He didn't respond. Mr. Brown returned the tape back to its cardboard case. I walked a few steps closer to the armchair.

"And I think you should stay," I said.

"Stay?" Mr. Brown said. "Didn't Jonathan tell you I don't even talk to people here?"

"You are talking to me now."

"Yeah, sure, in English," Mr. Brown said, and looked deflated.

"I don't think it's just about the language," I said.

"It's late," Mr. Brown said and tried to end the conversation. "You should go."

I didn't move.

"What about Mrs. Brown's wish?" I asked. "Don't you want to honor it? Maybe I can help?"

"Please, Marie," Mr. Brown nearly shouted. "You don't

understand and you can't help me. It's been forty-three years. Can't you hear how ridiculous it sounds? Forty-three years and I still hardly talk to people here. I love this town. And I've tried, but it didn't work. Maybe Jonathan's right. How can I feel this is where I belong when I can't even communicate? Now do you understand? Nobody can help me."

I stood there, stunned. I thought, *maybe you didn't try hard enough.*

Then I thought of Father.

After Mother died, Father suffered from severe insomnia and was eventually diagnosed with endogenous depression. I was young; I didn't understand. I thought Father was just sad. The evening before he died, Father said that he was going to terminate the future sessions with his psychiatrist. He thought no one could help him, but I told him, maybe he just wasn't trying hard enough. Around midnight, Father threw himself off the roof. Three days later, he died in the hospital from an intracranial injury.

I would not make the same mistake again.

I would not.

Today I spent the whole afternoon moving the furniture around, trying to find a new look for my room. As a result, my bed is now under the skylight. I lay in bed and stared at the cropped sky. My eyes followed an aeroplane flying from one corner to another, but all I could think about was Rachid kissing me last night.

Around noon yesterday, a cover of Arvo Pärt's *Für Alina* played by a musician friend of mine, Lars Skulberg from *Fredrikstad,* had just begun when the phone rang. I decided to ignore the ringing. I met Lars while he was on an exchange program at the conservatory in *Antwerpen,* and he spent a few months working in a café nearby my apartment. I remember the funny hat he always wore; it looked really special on him. Lars told many stories, and while they were all intriguing, I found the one with him taking a ferry to school as a daily routine truly remarkable. It made me fall in love with a place I had never been. Before he returned to *Fredrikstad,* Lars recited a scene from Heiner Müller's *Die Hamletmaschine* and gave me a CD.

The phone rang again.

"This is Rachid," a male voice spoke on the other end of the line. "May I speak to Marie?"

I was more curious about the reason Rachid was phoning rather than how he got my number. He said Principal Seynaeve asked him to organize a speech contest for immigrant children in three weeks, and he was wondering if we would be interested in catering the lunch – nothing fancy, just some bread, ham and cheese, drinks and some desserts. Later in the evening, I went over to Principal Seynaeve's school to meet Rachid. He thought it was nicer to discuss the details face to face.

When I arrived at the school, it was dark and there was no sign of people. I was looking for my phone when I heard Rachid's yell.

"Over here, Marie!" he shouted.

I followed the voice and saw Rachid, waving. His cellphone provided a faint light source, at the far end of the building. He looked rather energetic. Before I reached the corner, Rachid disappeared into the dark. I thought, *he sure knew how to entice me,* when I slipped into the dark after him. Though I wasn't afraid, I couldn't see my own hands, so

I called out for Rachid.

All of a sudden, the lights outside the building came on and blinded me for a few seconds. When I could see clearly again, I realized I was standing in the school parking lot, and in the middle of the parking lot there was a table. I walked to the table and saw there was a white cake on it. The icing was not evenly spread, and the shape was not exactly round. I had no clue where Rachid was. I let my imagination run wild before he reappeared from the dark, walking towards me. I could see he was holding something.

"Happy Birthday, Marie," Rachid said smilingly and gave me the things he was holding: a bucket of chicken from KFC and a bottle of red wine. I was surprised, I mean, like, *surprised.*

"How did you…? When did you…?" I stuttered.

"Welcome to the twenty-first century," Rachid said. "You can find out pretty much anything these days if you want to."

"But why?" I asked in awe.

"Well," he said, "I thought I'd drive to The Netherlands to get a bucket of your favorite food, make you a cake, and throw you an outdoor surprise party just so you can properly apologize to me for thinking I was just another foreigner."

"Please don't remind me," I said. "I feel so embarrassed already."

"I was kidding," he said. "I just wanted to do something nice for you."

Don't get me wrong, he is a nice young man, but the age difference was hard to ignore. Rachid confessed he didn't actually make the cake. His sixteen-year-old sister made it after he told her he was planning to impress a girl. I don't remember the last time someone called me a *girl.* We ate a third of the cake and drank half the bottle of wine. Rachid suggested we go out, but I expressed my concerns and told him I needed time to think about it.

Before I got into my car, Rachid asked if he could kiss me.

I said okay.

A package from New York arrived today. It was from Mr. Brown. Four months ago, the Browns officially left this town. Or were they sent away like a group of unwanted orphans? I couldn't tell. The Browns didn't celebrate their new future by inviting the people in town for a farewell party, and the town didn't give them an honorable goodbye either. It was as if they had never been here. I was looking for the scissors when I thought of a special experience I once had back in my youth.

One morning when I was on my way to school, I saw a white stone lying in the middle of the sidewalk. I stood in front of it and wondered how it had got there. I looked around and noticed a big pile of white stones on the opposite side of the road. The stone in front of me looked lonely on its own, so I decided to move it and bring it across the road to that pile of stones. I spent a long time trying to find a safe spot, among the pile of stones, for the stone. It didn't work. For some reason, the stone kept rolling down and falling back to the ground, away from the group. I kept trying.

After a while, the stone seemed more stable sitting between a few stones. Though it was still wobbly, it stopped rolling. I was satisfied and thought the hard work had paid off. Before I continued on my way to school, I looked over to the other side of the road. I must not have paid any attention when I lifted the stone because there was a hole where the stone had been. The hole was not huge but it was big enough for people to trip over. I then picked up the stone again and put it back where I found it, where it belonged.

Inside Mr. Brown's package, there were two items: a book and a VHS tape. I was right; Mr. Brown is the poet I Googled. The book, titled *The Important Equal the Irrelevant,* is a collection of Mr. Brown's poems that were published between 1961 and 1969. Apparently he stopped writing poetry after Jonathan was born. Nevertheless, according to the web-link I found, Mr. Brown did continue publishing his poetry back in Indiana all the way till the late eighties. The publisher went bankrupt soon after they published Mr. Brown's sixth book. Mr. Brown's talent was never recognized again and his writing career ended. I opened the book and found two handwritten words on the first page:

To Marie

It took me a while to find the VHS player in the attic before I could bring it down and connect it to the TV. There was no picture for the first minute. The anticipation was killing me. The first thing that came on screen was an empty white wall. A moment later, Mr. Brown entered in his blazer with the suede elbow pads. Mr. Brown came to a halt when he arrived at the center of the frame. He turned, faced the camera and slowly began to speak. The talk was given in the dialect from this town. Word for word, Mr. Brown took his time.

I smiled at every word. I smiled.

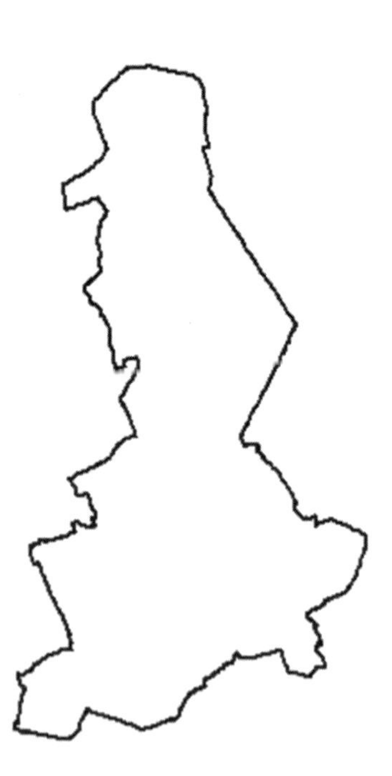

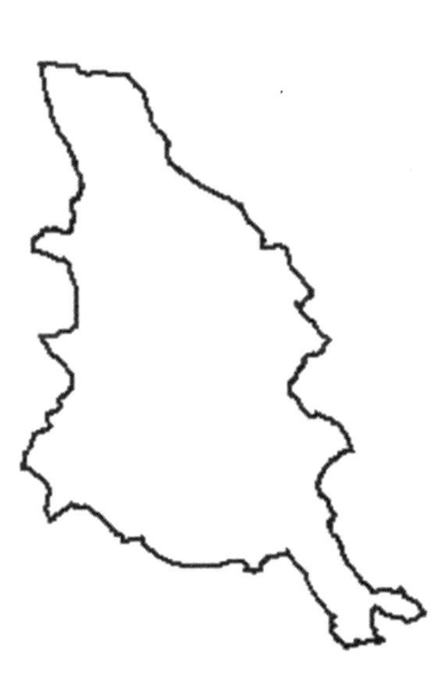

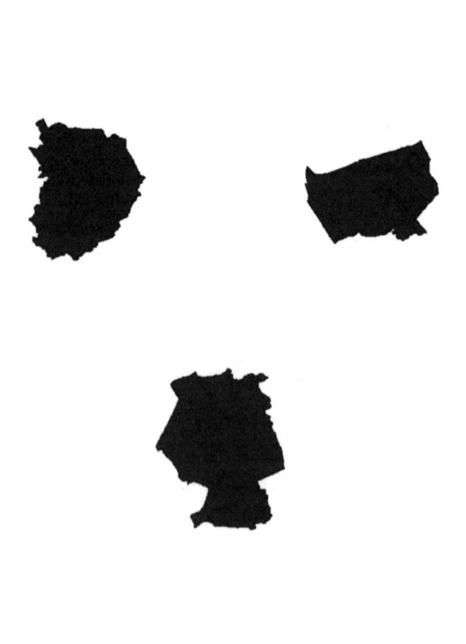

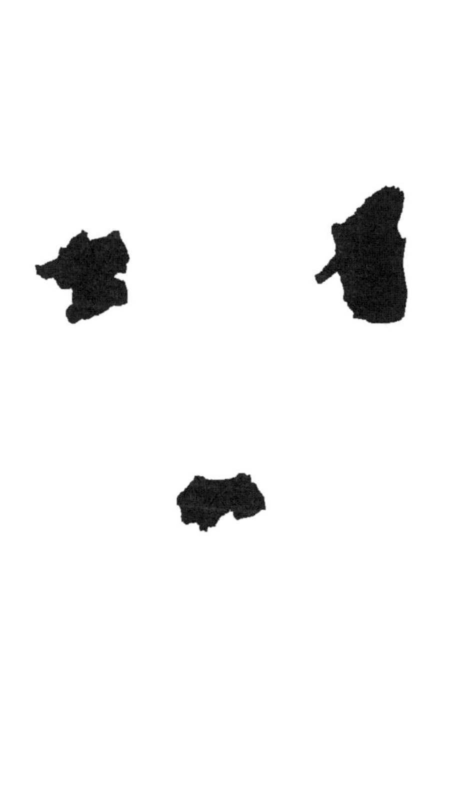

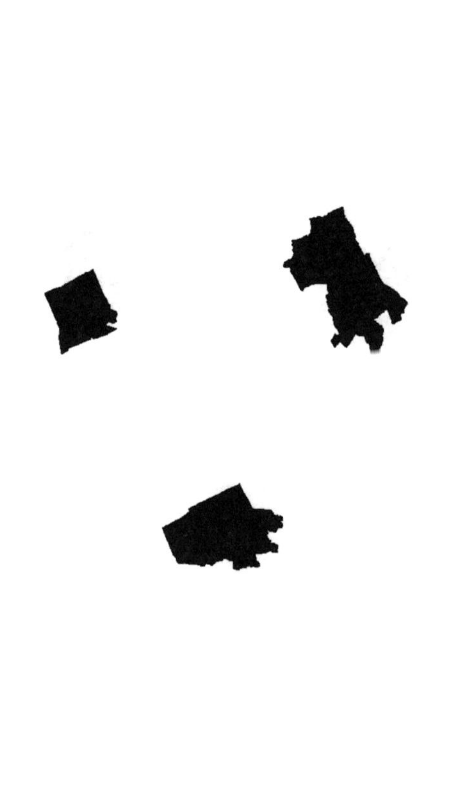

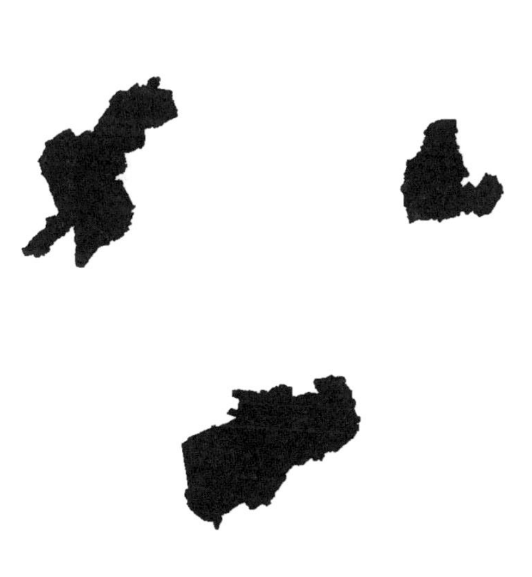

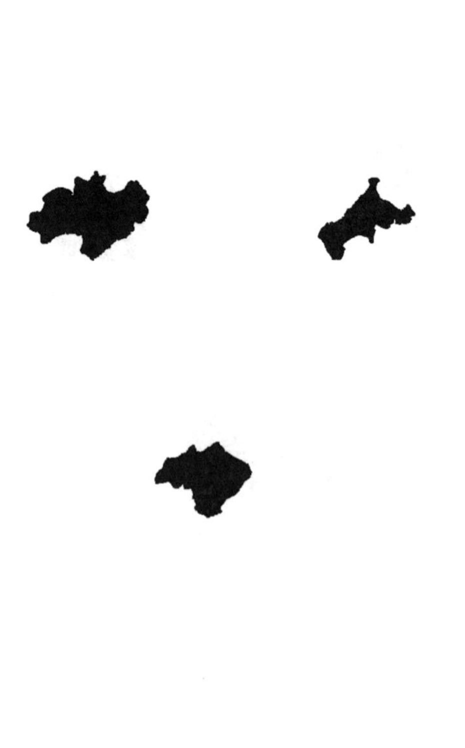

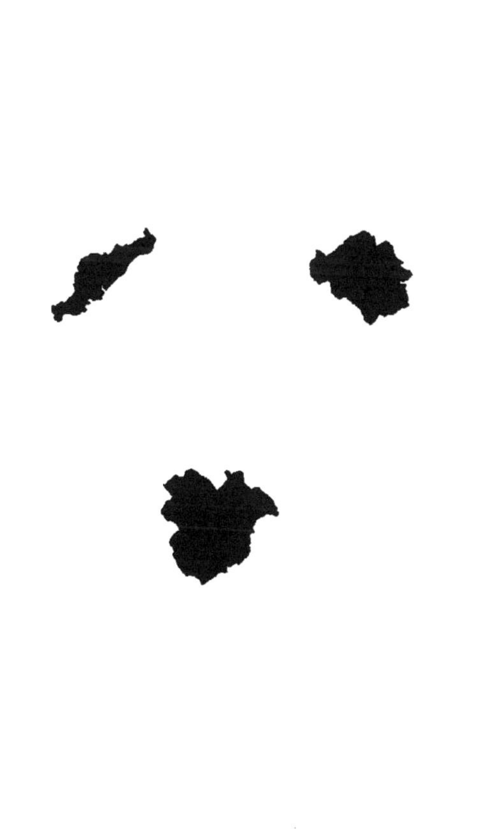

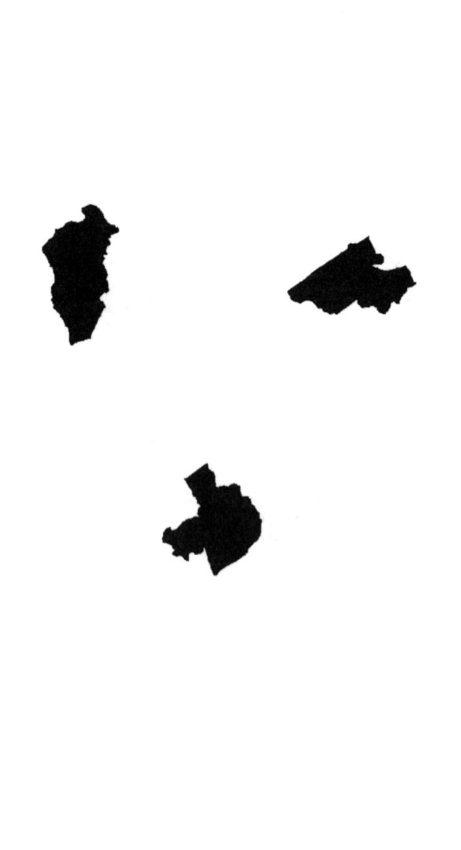

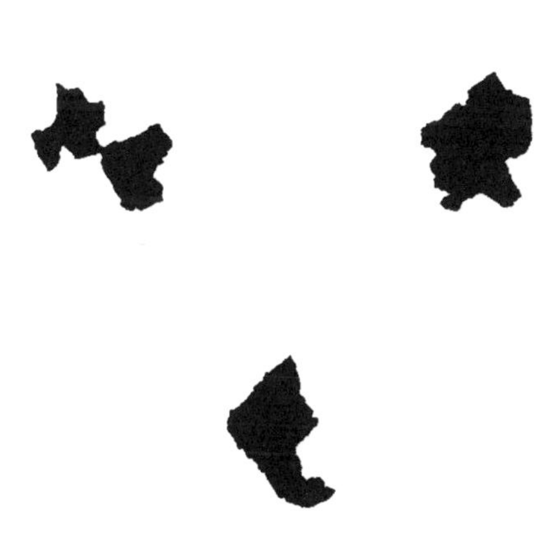

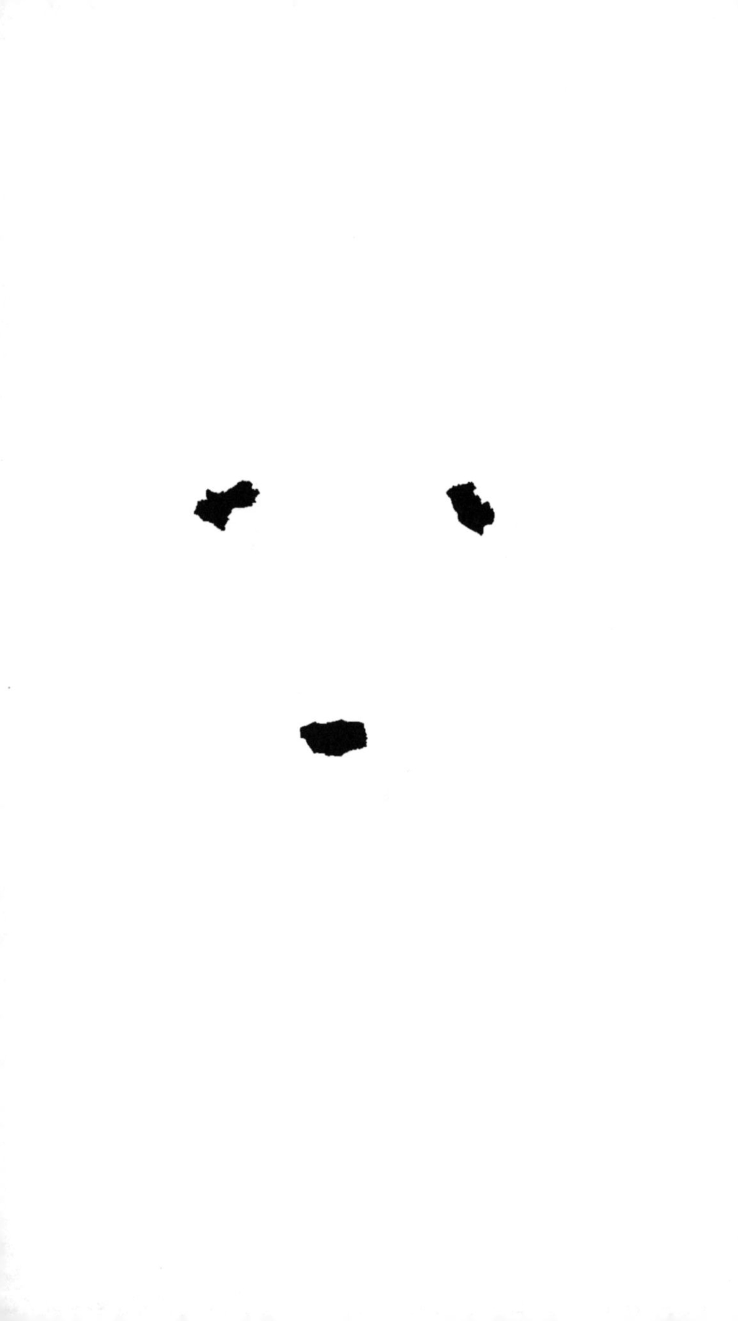

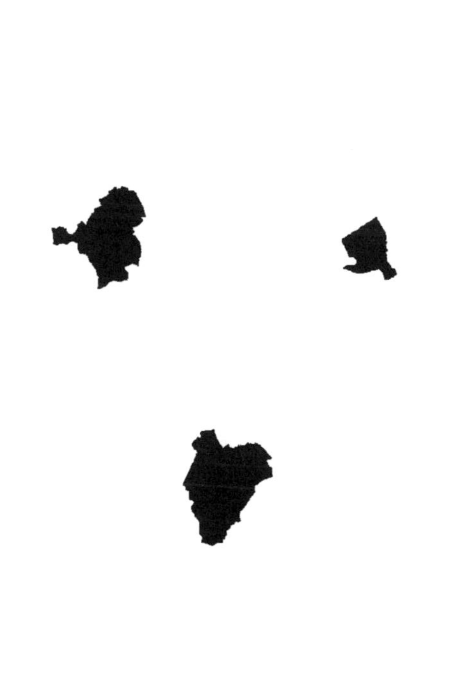

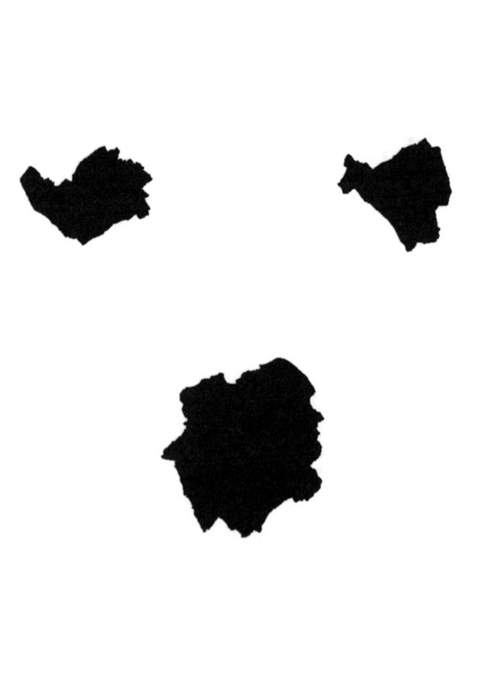

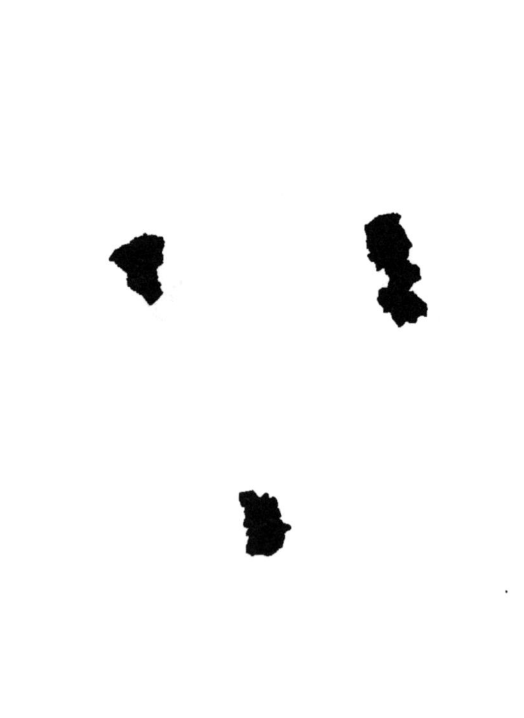

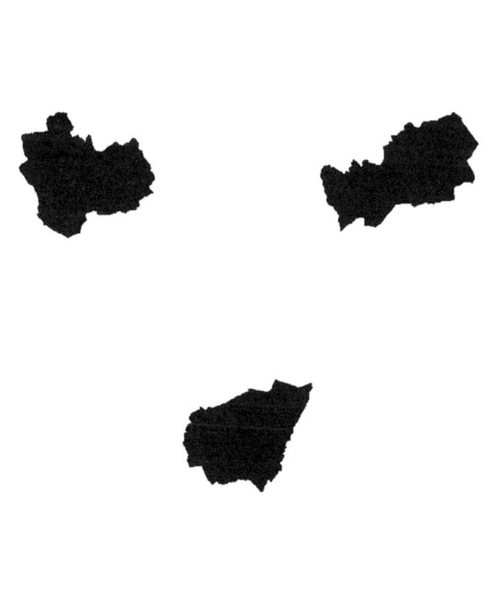

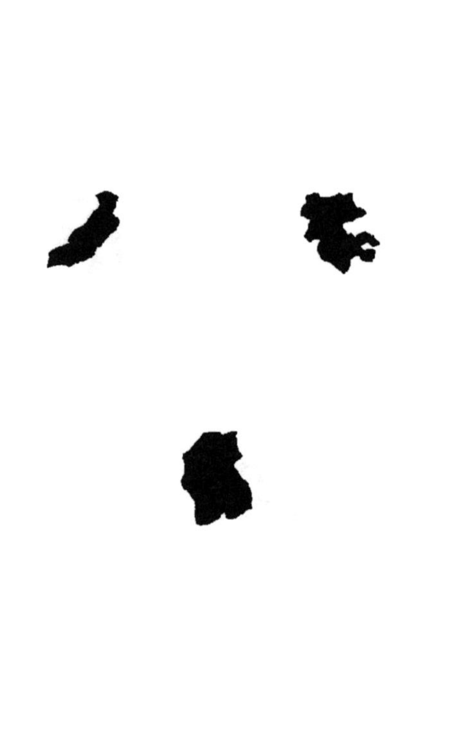

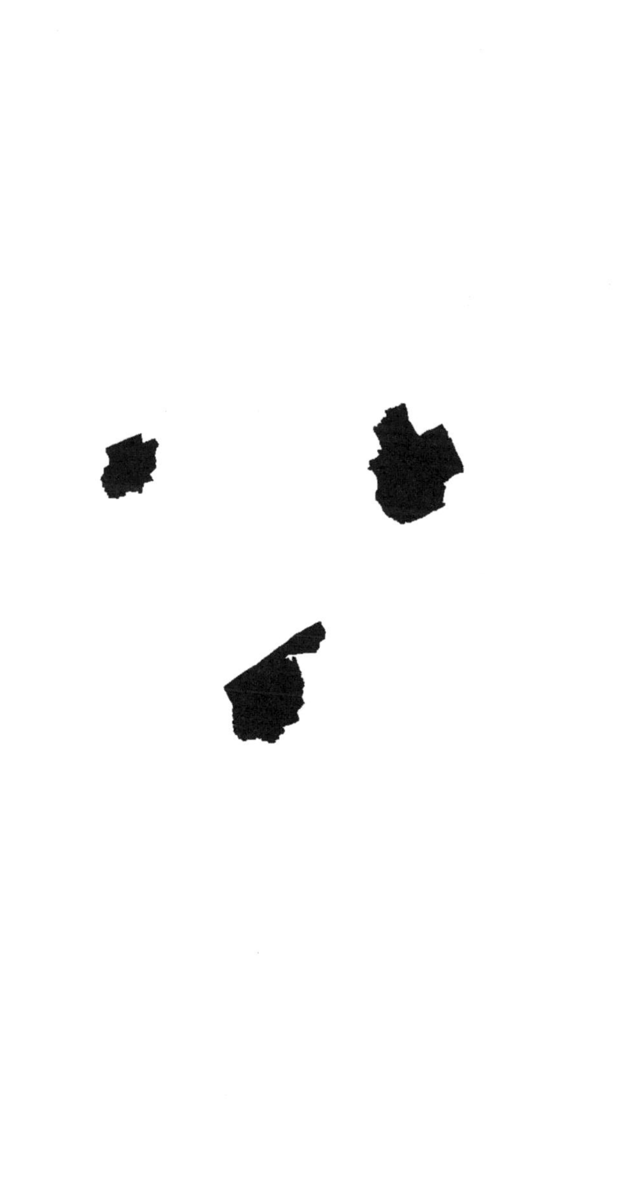

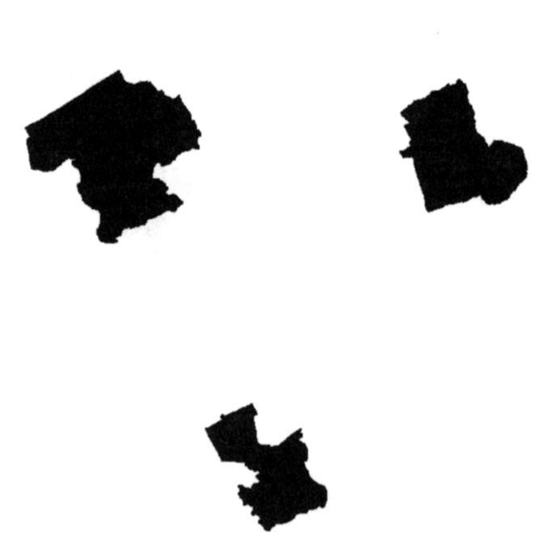

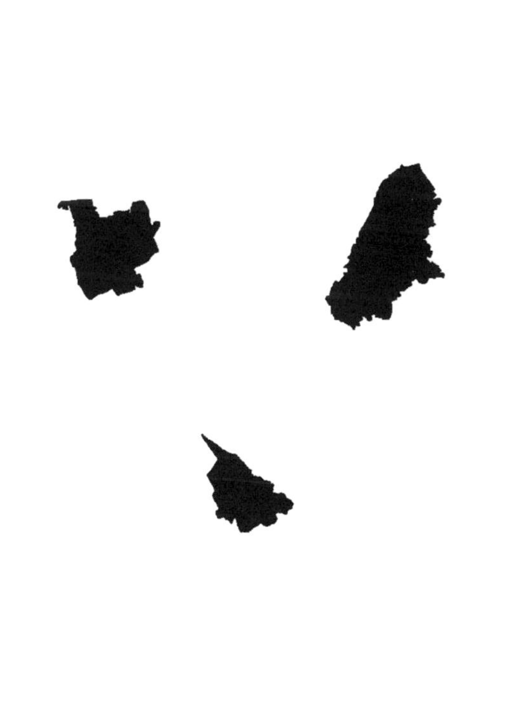

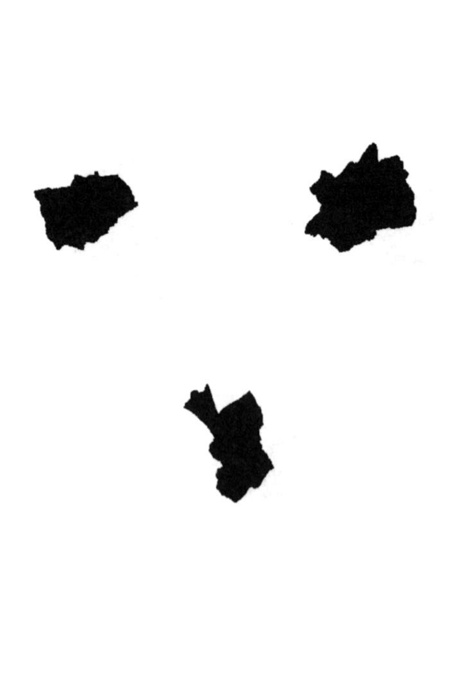

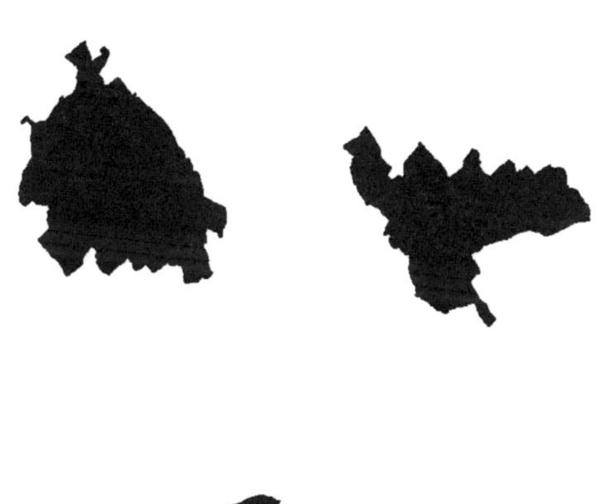

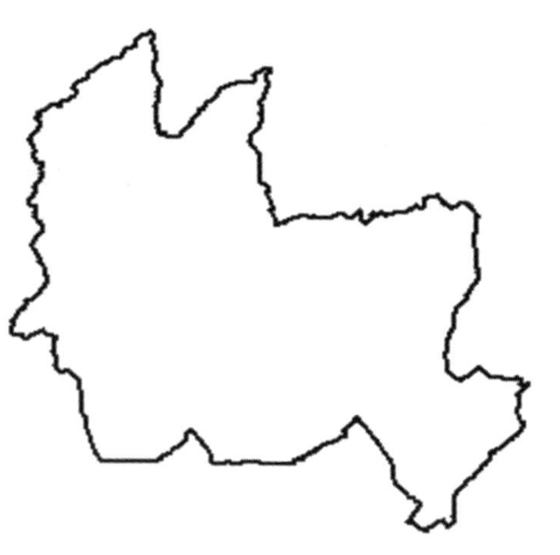

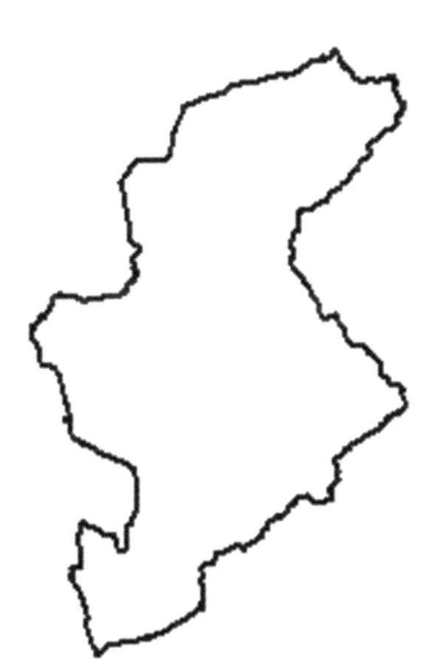

PART TWO

Jonathan Brown

The year 1987 was the year that Ronald Reagan challenged Mikhail Gorbachev to tear down the Berlin Wall, and the *Christelijke Volkspartij* won the Belgian general elections for the Chamber of Representatives and Senate. But for me, it was the year I left town. Mother cried when we said goodbye, but she knew if I stayed it would be for her and not for me. Mother always wanted me to be happy.

I was in my 4 p.m. meeting when my cellphone went off three times. Later I saw it was Father who had called. It's very unusual for him to call me at all, let alone at this hour. In the voice mail Father left identical messages for each call, "Mother died."

I called Father and told him we would fly back as soon as possible. On the telephone, Father explained that Mother had collapsed on the street after she stepped out of a grocery store. They did the shopping in the afternoon together, but Mother went back to the store for a second time to get more cheese. Father loves cheese. Rebecca offered to accompany me back to Belgium. She said it'd be nice for Father to finally meet her, and his grandson. We decided to take Jimmy out of school for two weeks in case we were needed longer there. I haven't been back in years, but I guess the town is still the town, and Father is still Father.

What was Grandma Anne like? Jimmy started playing twenty questions after we were seated in the plane.

"Well, she was the bravest woman I've ever known," I said and tried to recall memories of Mother. "And she raised Father on her own."

I didn't really mean that and of course it wasn't true.

"How come I've never met her?" Jimmy continued.

"You actually have, but you were too little to remember," I answered, and this time I didn't lie.

"Did she bring me presents?" Jimmy asked.

"Yes," I answered. "She put three kisses on your tiny nose."

"I wish I remember that she did that," Jimmy commented and turned his attention to the lights outside the aircraft.

I remember Mother's three kisses on my nose. She did it whenever I fell down. Mother always said three was her lucky number because there were three of us.

Mother met Father when she was studying at Indiana University back in the late sixties. Studying abroad was an extraordinary thing to do at the time, for a woman from her town, and Mother was really proud of it. Not so long after Mother arrived in the States, she met Father at a book camp. Father was a small town writer writing poems for a local publisher. Mother's childhood dream was to become an author, so when she met Father it was love at first sight. I've often wondered if I killed Father's creativity since he seemed to have stopped writing after I was born. When I read Father's works, it felt like I was reading words that were written by a stranger whose soul I didn't know. Though it was hard for me to link Father to those good writings, Mother used to say that they were exactly why she was so attracted to Father. Apparently, it was amazing to Mother that a person like Father could write nothing but graceful words.

After three days at the book camp, neither of them could go anywhere without the other. They were madly in love. Mother used to tell me about the many romantic things Father did for her at the beginning of their relationship. I always listened and thought, where did that Father go? For as long as I can remember, Father has never once performed any romantic gestures for Mother. Well, at least not that I know of. But I guess I should believe Mother, otherwise how could she stay with Father for more than forty years? On the seventh day after they met, Father proposed. And Mother said yes. That was January twenty-third, 1968. A few weeks later, Father moved from Schnellville to South Bend, Indiana. I have never been to Schnellville, nor have I ever thought of going. The town, according to Wikipedia, only has a population of 170. How they managed to support a local publisher I will never know. Mother said Father was born for towns like that because he was the kind of person who not only enjoyed, but also embraced, solitude – both physically and mentally. And I bet he still does.

"It is just how your father is," Mother explained. "It's his personality."

Although I hardly remember Father ever expressing his love for Mother, whenever I challenged her regarding this matter, Mother always won the argument by talking about the most courageous thing Father had ever done for her.

The year after they were married, I was born. Mother suggested that we stay in Indiana for the first few years, and when I was a bit older we could go back and live in West Flanders for another few years. Father was not really convinced by the idea, but Mother thought that way I would get to learn both cultures and languages. The plan went faster than Father had anticipated. When I was nearly one, Mother's father fell ill and needed someone to look after him. Since Mother had no other siblings, going back seemed to be the only option for her. Mother asked Father for his thoughts, and Father, surprisingly, didn't seem at all hesitant. He told Mother: I guess we'll just have to go back. Three weeks later, we moved back to West Flanders. It was 1970. When I was growing up, Mother used to repeatedly stress how big a man Father was for moving back for her father. I often thought Mother told those stories so I wouldn't think of Father as a man who didn't care.

Both cabin lights and fasten-seatbelt lights were switched on when the captain announced that we would be landing in about twenty-five minutes. The weather was partly cloudy, and we could expect showers in the afternoon.

"Are we here? Are we here?" Jimmy pushed his face against the window and asked. I fastened my seatbelt first before I fastened Jimmy's. Rebecca rested her head on my shoulder and told me she could tell I was nervous. I wished I could tell her she was imagining things.

We arrived at Father's house, my old home, a few hours later than we expected. Father called my cell a few times, but I was busy dealing with people from the car rental company. The last time I drove a car in Belgium was more than twenty years ago and that was also the last time I drove a non-automatic. The company claimed that they did have automatics, which I highly doubted, but they were all rented out and all they had left were stick shifts. I hadn't gotten to the town yet and I was already disappointed.

The rental is a Volvo. Father drove Volvos. The thing about driving a stick shift is that you have to collaborate with the clutch to switch gears. Some men find it more masculine to drive this way. I think it's a waste of time.

Automobiles were probably the only thing Father and I had in common. As soon as I turned eighteen, all I could think about was getting my driver's license and driving away from my life. People used to tell me that I've got nothing to complain about. Father was not a drunk, nor a gambler, and Mother was a loving and terrific mother, but I had my reasons just as all other teenagers did. I used to sneak into the garage when Father was out to the grocery store with Mother. That was the only time I could get my hands on Father's car magazines. Strangely enough, Father seemed to be taking better care of his magazines than of the actual car. Someone could throw a pie onto the windshield of his car without worrying about Father getting angry, but if you dared to smudge one page of those magazines – well, you would be sorry.

In my memories, Father was home a lot. As a young child I didn't find it odd until Jan, a boy in my fourth grade, asked about Father's occupation. I told him Father didn't work. Jan didn't believe me and called me a liar, and I went home crying. I never had the courage to confront Father, but I always remember the day I was called a liar because of him. Later when I was older, I discovered that Mother, during all those years, had worked fulltime at the town hall and part-time as a seamstress. But I would say Mother actually had three jobs. Being Father's translator certainly qualified as her third job.

Father was waiting outside by the street when our car pulled up to the house, and apparently Father also noticed the awkward way I was driving.

"You didn't ask for an automatic?" Father asked.

"Sorry we're late," I said and ignored Father's sarcastic question.

Father seemed a bit nervous when Rebecca and Jimmy stepped out of the car. Jimmy was hiding behind Rebecca when she introduced Father to him.

"Jimmy," Rebecca said and pushed Jimmy forward, "this is your Grandpa Jeff."

Father was holding a white teddy bear, but he didn't seem to remember to give it to Jimmy.

"Is that for Jimmy?" Rebecca reminded Father.

"What?" Father responded and looked at the teddy bear. "Oh yes, it's for Jimmy."

Jimmy accepted the teddy bear and hid behind Rebecca again. Father didn't mind, and he turned around and headed into the house. We followed Father in. I told him that after tomorrow, we would move to a hotel in a neighboring town. He didn't object. I walked into my old bedroom, and it still looked the same, like I had never left. Father said Jimmy could sleep in my old room, and for Rebecca and me he prepared the guest room.

"It's *Willy and Wanda!*" Jimmy shouted in excitement when he pointed at the wall. "But the names are different, Su... Sus... Ke..."

"*Suske en Wiske,*" I said. "Remember Daddy told you it was originally a Belgian comic?"

"Why is it framed?" Jimmy asked.

"Well," I explained, "that is because it's very important to Daddy."

"Was it a present from Grandma Anne?" Jimmy asked.

"No," I said and thought of how I got it. "It was from Grandpa Jeff."

It was two weeks before I turned eight. Mother told me we could only have a little celebration for my birthday that year, according to a new rule set by the mayor, but I knew it was because we didn't have much money. I wasn't going to complain. I was never a spoiled kid. I understood our family situation, especially since Father wasn't working.

Jan's father owned a big farm so he always had the latest issues of *Suske en Wiske.* He would let me read them for free if I did his math homework for him. Jan wasn't very smart.

A week before my birthday, I came home late one evening, twenty-five minutes past my curfew. I knew I was in trouble. Father never appreciated me being out after dark and he was upset. I explained, but Father didn't seem to agree with how I justified my actions. I was grounded for two weeks. A sudden rage came over me after hearing the unfair punishment. I pleaded with Father – if I had my own comic books then I wouldn't be home late after doing Jan's stupid homework, and I wouldn't have to beg to read comic books. I slammed my door in Father's face. In the next few days I didn't talk to Father. I didn't even see him around much.

On the afternoon of my birthday, before Mother was home, Father told me to go upstairs and check my desk. When I walked into my room, I saw the latest issue of *Suske en Wiske* lying on my desk, and next to it was a few hundred franks. And on top of the money there was a note:

I know it won't last forever, but nothing does.
Don't stress about things you don't have –
you're better than that.
But once a year, go ahead and enjoy your birthday.

The note was not signed, but I could tell by the handwriting that it was from Father. When Mother was cutting the cake, I asked her how Father had managed to give me the comic book and the money. Mother said that for the past week, Father had been working as an additional help at Jan's father's cattle farm. Father cleaned and put new food in the troughs. That was the Father I knew, thirty-three years of age with no steady job. But whenever he did nice things like this for me, I was immediately won over.

I later found a crappy frame for the comic book, and I kept the money in a drawer for years. I slept in my old bed with Jimmy this night, a little crammed but it was fine.

I saw Marie Vandenberghe today at the grocery store I used to go to. Father didn't feel like leaving the house, so he asked if I could go to the store for him. The milk was running low. I took Father's car, thinking it might be more comfortable, but I was wrong. I forgot Father's car always had this awful smell of cigarettes. Not that I don't smoke. I just don't like smoking inside a car, especially not with the windows closed. And I thought Mother said Father had quit.

Marie was in the little room at the back of the store when I was there. I could see her every now and then through the half-open door. She seemed busy, so I didn't bother her. At the cashier I asked the lady about Mrs. Maes, Marie's aunt, and if she could send her my regards. The lady told me that Mrs. Maes had died at the beginning of this year, and now the store belonged to Marie.

Marie's mother, Mrs. Vandenberghe, tried inviting us over for dinner a couple of times when we moved back to town, only Father refused on every occasion. Eventually she got the hint, and we were never invited again. Because of Father, we didn't have much, if any, social interaction with the locals. Mother was born and raised here, but she felt guilty if she went out without Father. Mother was that considerate. In the end, Mother's childhood friends contacted her less and less. I didn't, and still don't, understand how Father could lead such an isolated life, and how Mother could let him. But life went on, and we survived.

I tutored Marie once when she was in her first year of secondary school. On a Sunday afternoon, Mrs. Vandenberghe came to the house with some *beuterkoeken* and asked Mother if I could help Marie with her French. I overheard the conversation and that Mrs. Vandenberghe was going to offer me twenty franks for tutoring Marie twice a week. With that money I could get one new comic book every week. I jumped in and sealed the deal with Mrs. Vandenberghe before Mother answered for me. The third time I went to tutor her, Marie kept asking me to say something in an American accent. I felt insulted, so I got up and left. The next day, Mother brought me back to Mrs. Vandenberghe's house to apologize for my behavior. Mrs. Vandenberghe offered to pay me for the lessons I'd given, but Mother didn't think I deserved it. And I never went back again. A year later, Mrs. Vandenberghe passed away. Mother expressed that it would be thoughtful if we went to the funeral. Father didn't want to sit in the crowd, so we stood in the back. When they carried thc coffin out of the church, I saw Mr. Vandenberghe, with tears in his eyes, marching ahead. Marie was walking next to Mrs. Maes. They were both crying. I looked away. And the following year, I left for the States.

The lady at the cashier asked if I would like to talk to Mrs. Maes' niece. I explained that I was in a hurry and kindly refused. Before I was out of the store, with my hand on the doorknob, I suddenly had the realization that this was the last door Mother had entered and exited. I thought of the last time I held Mother's hand.

Huize Rossetti was located a few kilometers outside *Gistel.* Although it had a radiant charm, the hotel looked more like a bed and breakfast than a regular hotel. Thanks to its discreet nature, even with a GPS we couldn't find it, so I had to call the hotel. Rebecca was quite excited when she found *Huize Rossetti* on the Internet. Born Irish American in New Jersey and later moving to New York City, Rebecca was no stranger to Italian culture. Sometimes she even preferred Italian hot dogs to shepherd's pies. Although you probably can only find Italian hot dogs in New Jersey – I'm not sure. Mrs. Rossetti was standing outside on the street, talking to me on the phone, when she told me she saw us. Shortly after, I noticed a voluptuous fifty-something woman waving at us joyfully. Mrs. Rossetti yelled that the parking and the reception were at the back of the house, so I followed her instructions and went around the corner. There were no other cars parked in the parking lot. It was obvious we were the only guests.

Jimmy was already asleep in the car when we arrived at the hotel. Rebecca greeted Mrs. Rossetti and carried Jimmy up to the room. While Mrs. Rossetti was checking us in, I looked around the reception. The decor was very Italian, and also very red. Mrs. Rossetti had immigrated to West Flanders from Savigliano, Italy, a few years ago after she and her husband had both retired. I had never heard of Savigliano, but I guessed she had never heard of my hometown either. *Why West Flanders?* I bet people asked her all the time, so I decided to spare Mrs. Rossetti from having to answer the question for the hundredth time.

After we'd settled down in the room, Mrs. Rossetti rang and asked if we fancied some supper. Jimmy was running a bit of a temperature, so Rebecca decided to stay in the room and look after him.

"Just bring me some left overs," Rebecca said.

I went downstairs to the dining room and found Mrs. Rossetti busy setting the table. She said I could bring the pasta sauce to the table when I offered to help. Mrs. Rossetti apologized when she served the food on my plate.

"I am very sorry, normally we have an Italian chef here," she explained, "but he is now on holiday for two weeks."

Mrs. Rossetti was being humble. Her homemade ravioli served with homemade pasta sauce tasted way better than a forty-five-dollar ravioli dish I once had in an Italian restaurant on Fifth Avenue. New York City should be ashamed. Mrs. Rossetti poured herself a glass of red wine and sat down across from me. She asked me if we were Americans, judging from the accent. I told her I was half American, half West Flemish and Jimmy was one-fourth of each. Rebecca was born and raised in the States, but her grandfather was Irish.

"Hey, and I am one-eighth German," Mrs. Rossetti said proudly.

"I see," I said and put a piece of ravioli in my mouth. "Seems like no one is one-hundred-percent of anything these days."

"It's better this way," Mrs. Rossetti commented and took a sip of her wine. "No?"

"Well, I should hope so."

"You should have seen my grandmother," Mrs. Rossetti added. "She was gorgeous."

Out of the blue, a question struck my mind. I wondered if Mrs. Rossetti spoke the local language.

"Do you speak Flemish, or West Flemish, Mrs. Rossetti?"

"Yes, I do," she said. "Why?"

I said I was just curious, and then I told her about Father. Mrs. Rossetti said my story reminded her of an Icelandic couple she knew back in Italy. The couple lived in Savigliano for twenty years and never spoke any Italian, but they had a daughter who grew up multilingual, and when the daughter turned seven she began to be her parents' translator.

"Maybe her and my mother could have been friends," I said. "Do they still live there?"

"I think so, yes," Mrs. Rossetti said.

I told her that I was going to ask Father to come and live with us in the States. Mrs. Rossetti didn't seem to think Father would agree. She thought forty-three years in Belgium was a long time. Maybe like her friends back in Savigliano, Father wouldn't think of leaving. I told Mrs. Rossetti that her friends still had each other and their daughter, but Father had lost both his wife and his translator.

"And you? You've never thought of moving back here?" Mrs. Rossetti asked.

"Me? Well, my life is over there."

"Your father might tell you the same," Mrs. Rossetti said.

"More wine?"

"No, no," I said. "Thanks, though."

Before I went upstairs, we spoke in Flemish for a bit, just for the fun of it. Mrs. Rossetti's Italian accent was enchanting. I thought about what she said about how Father might respond to my invitation. I wondered if Mrs. Rossetti was right.

How many times a day do you think of committing suicide? I once asked this question to my college roommate, Danny Wallace, and his answer was refreshing. "Zero," he said. Two weeks before graduation, Danny hanged himself.

Jimmy was feeling better, so Rebecca took him out for an early walk in the fields. I decided to stay in and take a bath. As the tub was filling up, I thought of Danny. I asked the question because I used to think of killing myself at least once a day. Honestly, I wouldn't be able to give any sensible reason why I thought of committing suicide so often. But every morning while I was lying in the tub, I thought about it. People told me suicide was the stupidest and most irresponsible thing in the world, but as a teenager I found it the bravest commitment on earth.

When Grandpa Luc, Mother's father, died, Father had the idea that Mother might do something silly. I thought Father was being paranoid. But soon, a new house rule was introduced:

NO LOCKING THE DOORS.

We could close them but not lock them. When Mother spent a little longer in the shower, Father would be by the door asking if everything was okay. He would go back to check on Mother again if she didn't come out a few minutes later. Mother thought Father was being caring, and she told Father she would never do anything to hurt us. Luckily, Father's worry did not come true.

I called Father around ten and asked if he needed any help since the funeral was tomorrow. He said a man, Hans, from Marie's store, had volunteered to assist. Everything seemed to be taken care of. After lunch, I phoned Father again and asked the same question. Father gave the same answer. I called Father two more times this evening and heard the same words from him two more times. Perhaps I am a bit worried about Father too.

I woke up five minutes before the alarm clock went off. I told Rebecca I wanted to see Father before the funeral, so she and Jimmy could come later by taxi. I got in the rental and drove off. The skies, the birds and even the unoccupied crane by the construction site next to the hotel all looked so serene. I thought of Grandpa Luc's funeral. It was also held on such a day.

Father was already in the living room, busy getting the food and the drinks ready on the tables when I arrived. The arrangement in the living room was a bit odd. Father had put all the tables to one side of the room and all the chairs to the other. I didn't bother asking why. Father always had his reasons for doing things a certain way. I was instructed to move a few chairs to the hallway next to the living room entrance. Father thought the smoking area could be there since we would be serving food in the living room, and because it was like four degrees outside. I must admit I didn't expect Father to be so organized and calm. I was expecting to see him in a more disoriented state. I mean, he had just lost his wife. But I now remembered that one of Father's strengths was keeping things to himself.

After Father was satisfied with the work we had done, he went upstairs to change. A while later, Father came downstairs wearing a dashing black suit. I recognized the suit from an old family photograph I once saw in Mother's drawer when Mother asked me to help her look for her keys. In the picture, Father was wearing the same suit he had put on today. He was smiling. Mother, who stood right next to Father in the picture, also smiling, was wearing a white gown and carried a child in her arms. It must be me. I looked no more than three years old. Mother said when she and Father got married they didn't have much money. Then with me being born and moving back here to take care of Grandpa Luc, they never had a proper wedding. So on my second birthday, Mother and Father decided to go on a simple honeymoon to *Blankenberge* and took a family portrait slash wedding photo in front of the *vuurtoren*. And for the first time in his life Father wore a suit. Mother thought he was the most handsome man in the world.

Around ten o'clock, Rebecca and Jimmy arrived at the house. We drove off to the cemetery. Father didn't think

Mother would like to have an overtly religious service, and I think he was right, so we invited people to attend only the burial. Some of Mother's old colleagues and school friends came, but Father didn't talk to any of them.

About half past eleven, we moved the group back to the house. Not everyone at the burial came to the reception. Rebecca thought it was a bit sad, but I guess Father expected as much. While I was greeting the guests, out of the corner of my eye I saw that Father was sitting in the hallway the whole time. I ran into Marie when I went to speak to Father, I called Rebecca and Jimmy over and introduced them to her. Before we moved on to other guests, I told Marie it was nice seeing her again after such a long time and that we should catch up later.

I advised Father to say something to thank the guests for attending. It was a very short speech, but I could tell it was the hardest thing for him to do. Only then did I start to picture what Father's life would be like without Mother, and I didn't like what I saw.

After the guests were gone, Rebecca brought Jimmy upstairs for a nap, and I stayed downstairs to clean up. While I was walking to get the chairs from the hallway, I saw cigarette smoke wafting past the living room door. *Who was smoking?* I thought. It was Father. I remembered the cigarette smell I'd encountered when I drove his car to the store the other day. I went and sat down next to Father.

There was a framed drawing hanging on the wall in front of us. I recognized it.

"When did you have it framed?" I asked.

"Some time after you left for New York," Father answered.

"I can't believe you had it framed."

"It was your mother's idea," Father said. "Everything you did was a treasure to her."

I looked at Father. I observed his profile and thought, *When did he get so old?* I turned my eyes back to the drawing.

"You remember what this drawing was supposed to be?" I asked.

Father didn't respond and puffed on his cigarette.

"It was an assignment from Mrs. Vanpaemel's class. She asked us to draw what our mothers do most for our fathers."

Father continued to puff on his cigarette.

"Mrs. Vanpaemel was fascinated by the concept of Mother being your translator all the time," I said and watched for Father's reaction.

Father put out his cigarette.

"Well, she didn't get it right away of course," I said and laughed. "She actually thought Mother was a social worker that helped people with special needs."

When Father lit another cigarette, I asked for one. We engaged in a somewhat unpleasant conversation regarding his future. Father didn't take the suggestion of coming back to live with us in New York very well. I said something, he said something – we almost had a fight. Unwilling to negotiate any further, Father concluded the discussion.

"I'm staying," Father said.

Later I was upstairs, by the bedroom window, getting Jimmy's toys back into his backpack when I saw Marie leaving the house through the backdoor in the kitchen. And judging from her sneaky way of walking, I knew she had heard the conversation.

Mrs. Rossetti gave us a wake-up call today. We didn't ask for it, but apparently my cellphone battery was dead when Father tried to reach me. He then called the hotel. Father left a message asking me to come over to the house and help him go through Mother's stuff. He wanted to get rid of a few things. I told Rebecca to take Jimmy to *Brugge* as planned. It is their first time in Belgium, and I want them to be able to see the place.

When I arrived at the house about a quarter past ten, Father was in Mother's walk-in closet upstairs. The closet, though narrow, was quite large considering the size of the house. Mother often found me asleep in there with a comic book in my hand.

Most of the stuff was already packed and put away in boxes. Father told me to do a final check before he sent them to *De Kringwinkel.* Standing inside the walk-in closet knowing Mother was gone felt really strange. The smell of Mother was left adrift like an abandoned child. I wondered if it cried at night.

There were empty hangers hanging on the rods. I noticed, judging from the number of boxes Father had stacked outside the dressing room, that the amount of hangers outnumbered the quantity of clothes Mother once owned.

"How come there are so many hangers and only three boxes of clothes?" I asked.

"Your mother collected them," Father said. "She liked the way they looked."

"Huh, so Mother was a hanger collector," I said and took one off the rods. "You're not packing them?"

"No," Father said. "They'll stay."

I put the hanger back and walked towards an old, yellowish box sitting behind the door. I carried it out of the room.

"What is this?" I asked.

"I found it in a corner when I was packing," Father answered. "Just some old tapes."

"Tapes? What kind of tapes? Did you watch them?"

"No," Father said, looking at me. "You think I should?"

"Of course!" I said. "Aren't you curious?"

We brought the box downstairs to Father's study. While Father was connecting the VHS player, I went through the box. The tapes were labeled by year: *1981, 2003, 1995, 1989,*

2007, and so on and so forth. There must have been more than twenty of them. Father took one that was labeled *1993* and put it in the player. When the picture came on, the first thing we saw was Mother standing in front of a white wall. I didn't recognize the wall. I guess Mother must have recorded it at work. Mother looked younger than her real age in the video, and she seemed completely composed as she began to talk. Mother spoke about her love for us, how Father should handle the finances when she was gone, and that she hoped we would never need to see the video. From what I saw, it looked like a will. Mother went on and said that she wished Father would find a way to overcome his fear of social interaction and that he would try and speak the language. Mother was worried about Father leading a lonely life. Before Mother finished her talk, Father stopped the video and took the tape out of the machine. He looked agitated.

"Why did you stop it?" I asked.

"We have seen enough," Father said and put the tape back in the box.

"Don't you think we should talk about what Mother said in the video?"

Father didn't respond.

"It seems like Mother was worried about you being alone here after she was gone."

"There's nothing to worry about," Father stated. "I'm fine, I've been fine all these years."

"That's because Mother was always with you," I said emphatically. "You are *not* fine, Father."

"I think you should go now," Father said and lifted the box. "I can take care of the rest myself."

"Here we go," I said. "When are you going to quit being a baby and grow up? Can't you see how much Mother was worried about you? We're all worried about you."

Father dropped the box on the table.

"If she really worried about me she wouldn't have left me like this. If she really worried about me she should've done something about it." Father talked hysterically. "If she really worried about me, she should've known I'd be lost without her."

"Don't try to blame it on Mother," I said. "She was a wonderful mother and a perfect wife. It was *you* who put yourself in this situation, you and you alone."

"Didn't I ask you to leave?" Father said.

The police called early this afternoon. Father had a melt down in Marie's store and was escorted home in a police vehicle. The officer said Father didn't want them to contact me, but they were worried about his mental state. I apologized on behalf of Father and went immediately to the house. I was concerned.

Father was holding a green cardigan in his hand when I found him sitting at the dining table in the kitchen. There were two grocery bags on the counter. Father said that when the police escorted him out of the store, he forgot the bags, and it was Marie who brought them to the house not so long ago. I probably should thank Marie for that in person.

"Are you okay?" I asked.

Father didn't respond. He was staring at the green cardigan.

"Was that Mother's?" I asked.

"Yes," Father said. "She was wearing it that day."

On the telephone, the officer told me that Father had pushed the lady at the cashier. Though she hit her head, she was not pressing charges. It was a misunderstanding. Apparently, the lady thought Father was some kind of mentally challenged person who couldn't speak normally. Father has never been violent, so I wondered what broke him.

"Since when do you hit women?" I asked as a joke.

Father looked at me with his upset eyes.

"Oh relax," I said. "I was only kidding. So tell me, why did you push her?"

"I panicked. She kept talking to me really fast, and then she grabbed my wallet."

"So you pushed her?" I asked.

"I told you," Father said. "I panicked."

"And you still think you want to stay here," I said.

Father's incident reminded me of a painful childhood memory. It was a hot summer day, and I was lying on the floor when I heard the bells of an ice cream truck touring the neighborhood. I ran upstairs shouting, "ICE CREAM! ICE CREAM!" I couldn't find Mother, so I dragged Father onto the street and ran after the truck. Besides asking us which kind of ice cream and how many scoops we desired, the man also tried to chitchat with Father. But he had a pretty strong local accent, so Father was having a hard time understanding him. I could see

Father was getting anxious and starting to stammer. In the meantime, more and more customers began to queue behind us, so I decided to put Father out of his misery. I spoke to the man in the local dialect.

"Two scoops of chocolate chip cookie each, please," I said. "And please excuse my father, he is an American. His dialect is not good."

Father mumbled, "Show-off" when the man complimented me for being a good son. On our way back to the house, we had nothing but ice cream in our mouths. I never spoke up for Father again. I was eight, and I was hurt. Was Father jealous of me? Did he feel humiliated? Either way, I thought I was helping him.

Yesterday I visited Marie at her store. I wanted to thank her for bringing Father's groceries to the house and also apologize for Father's behavior. I told Marie she was probably the closest thing to a friend I had in this town, so I was wondering if she wouldn't mind having a talk with me because I'd like to know her opinion about Father's situation. Marie was very understanding. She told me she could relate to what Father was going through. She had seen it first-hand with her father. I know how Mr. Vandenberghe died. Mother talked about it in one of the letters she wrote me. *What a tragic way to go,* I thought.

Marie was in the middle of work, so we arranged to talk later in the evening. She asked me to meet her at a café named Sokoke in *Oudenburg.*

"It's an African café," she said, "and the owner makes great coffee."

I hesitated a bit because I don't think I have ever been to any African cafés, but then again, I have never been to *Oudenburg* either. At seven, Jimmy requested a bedtime story. I couldn't disappoint him, so I read him one. But before I knew it, it was ten to eight when Jimmy finally fell asleep. I rushed out and headed to *Oudenburg.* The sky was very clear last night. I knew it was not possible, but the stars seemed to have changed after all these years. I couldn't find the one Mother used to wish on.

I was forty-five minutes late. Marie was chatting with a man at the bar when I walked in. I apologized and told her the reason why I was late. Marie introduced me to the man she was talking to. He was the owner of Sokoke and his name was Ruben. I was in the mood for some local beers, but Marie insisted I try Ruben's great coffee. There were two choices: one with a wine flavor and one with a citrus tone. Marie recommended the former, but I went for the citrus. She shrugged and made a funny face when I gave my order. While we were waiting for our coffees, I had the impression that Marie was exploring my face with her eyes. That was a bit unusual, and I hoped my face did not turn red.

The coffee was excellent like Marie had promised, and I really enjoyed its sophisticated aftertaste. The three of us chatted for a bit before Ruben excused himself and went to the back of the café. I guessed he realized Marie and I needed some privacy.

Marie asked about Father. I told her that Father was still a little bit on edge when I went to see him but got much better the day after. I also told her that I'd asked Father to come and live with the family in New York, but he refused. Marie thought it was a nice gesture and wondered why Father objected to the proposal. I couldn't give her any answers since Father didn't give me one. Marie took out a small, round, white case from her purse. She said she needed some lip balm because coffee tended to give her dry lips. Marie opened it and lifted it to my nose. The lip balm was pink, and it smelled like roses. Had she been this feminine before? I tried to recall. My image of Marie was always of her being a tomboy and being very competitive with the boys. From time to time you could catch Marie racing boys on the street, and when that happened you knew the boys were bothering her while she was jogging.

I watched her put the lip balm back in the purse and wondered when that skinny girl with a boyish haircut had become this fine-figured woman in front of me. I looked away and continued what I was saying.

I talked about Mother's tapes. I told Marie what was recorded and what I thought about the tapes. I said Mother's wish and worries proved my point that Father should not stay and live here alone, but Marie thought it was not fair to deny Father his place in this town just because he didn't speak the language. Marie was trying to say that nobody except Father had the right to decide where he belonged. Before leaving, she talked about this language school and suggested that I take Father there.

I already knew Father was going to hate the idea.

Jimmy requested for his bed to be moved closer to the lamp by the windows. I must have pushed the bed too hard; it hit the wall and the painting fell off and landed on the bed. After checking there were no damages anywhere on the painting, I kneeled on the bed and attempted to hang it back. I noticed a hole that was hidden by the painting before. I pressed my eye against the hole, but it was pitch-black on the other side, so I couldn't make out what was in the room next door. I wondered if Mrs. Rossetti knew about the hole. This strange discovery brought back memories of a place I once stayed at.

When I first went to New York City, I lived with a fifty-year-old man called Charles Corrigan for a short time in the West Bronx. Born to an Irish father and a Puerto Rican mother, Mr. Corrigan was a native of the Bronx, a self-declared writer and a practiced dreamer. His parents did quite well selling secondhand cars back in the sixties, and after they died Mr. Corrigan sold the company and bought an apartment building. He had never worked a day in his life. The first time we met, I told Mr. Corrigan I needed an address to apply for jobs, but I couldn't afford to rent a whole apartment. I explained that I had experience writing and editing the school paper, so perhaps I could be his proofreader, or editor, in exchange for the rent. Mr. Corrigan didn't want to waste a perfectly good vacant apartment on me. He offered to let me stay in the same apartment with him instead. I accepted the offer right on the spot.

Mr. Corrigan's writing desk stood in the middle of the living room. He said he liked to look at the wall outside his bedroom when he wrote. Mr. Corrigan seemed to write a lot, but after living in the apartment for three months, I still hadn't received any material to proofread or edit. I asked Mr. Corrigan about it, but he casually avoided the question and said there was no rush. On the morning of the following Tuesday, Mr. Corrigan drilled a hole on the wall outside his bedroom and moved his desk against it. Then he disappeared for the day. I hauled the desk aside and peeped through the hole.

Mr. Corrigan's bedroom was daintily lit. I slowly navigated my eyes down and saw five single beds standing next to each other. It was the strangest interior for a one-person bedroom I had ever seen. The beds were so meticulously made I couldn't tell which bed Mr. Corrigan actually slept in. *Did he switch beds every night?* I wondered. The next day, Mr. Corrigan placed eighty-nine pages of his writing on the floor outside my bedroom door. When I came home later that evening, the hole was filled and painted. And a couple of months later, I couldn't even identify where the hole had been anymore.

I moved out of Mr. Corrigan's apartment after I got accepted to NYU. Mr. Corrigan threw me a simple farewell party for just the two of us. Up until the end, I never saw any of the texts I edited for Mr. Corrigan get published. And I never asked about the beds either.

Rebecca and Jimmy were quite excited about going to the event at Marie's store. Marie told me about this baking contest that was started and organized annually by her baker, Sarah, when I called her this morning, asking if I could pick up the language school brochure. Marie said she'd been meaning to invite us, but she had been busy the past few days. I told her not to worry and thanked her for the invitation. When I arrived at the store, Marie was covered in flour, making dough. I didn't think she baked much. I told Marie that Rebecca would bring Jimmy to the event later, but I wouldn't be able to join them because I had plans with Father. I said perhaps I could talk about the school thing with Father. Marie seemed pleased to hear that and handed me the brochure.

I actually didn't have any plans with Father today. I just wasn't in the mood for loud cheering coming from parents praising their children's every move. I was planning to go to Sokoke.

Ruben was drying a glass when I walked into the café. I squinted my eyes when the sunlight bounced off the glass. I greeted Ruben and sat down at the four-person table, since I appeared to be the only customer. While waiting for my coffee, I looked around the café. It seemed different in daytime. There was a low bookshelf standing next to the entrance. I didn't think it was there last time. The bookshelf consisted of only two shelves, and there were about thirty books standing in it.

I left my seat to take a closer look and noticed they were all copies of the same book, *The Bridge of San Luis Rey* by Thornton Wilder. Some of them were newer, and some of them were really old. They were all published in different years and bought in different cities and countries. The one I had in my hand was acquired in Copenhagen and dated December 2007.

"Have you ever read the book?" Ruben asked and put my coffee down on the table.

I returned the book to the shelf and walked back to my seat. I saw that Ruben had placed the cup so that its handle was on my left-hand side. I am a lefty. How considerate of him.

"No," I said, "I'm not much of a reader."

Ruben didn't collect those books. He bought them from a secondhand bookstore in London four years ago. The bookstore was about to close down for good, so the owner, Mr.

Eddington, was practically giving everything away for nothing. Ruben paid just twenty pounds for thirty-one books.

Mr. Eddington told Ruben that the collection used to belong to a literature professor, Julian Dawson, whose lifelong research was devoted to Wilder. Dawson later became obsessed with Wilder's Pulitzer-winning novel after he spent two years living in Peru. He was drawn to the conceptual ideas the book presented and how it formulated a potentially cosmic answer. Dawson died the previous spring before his trip to Wilder's grave in Hamden, Connecticut. He was seventy eight. Dawson's son, Theodore, a stockbroker, inherited the collection but found it unattractive. And so the collection ended up in the bookstore.

"What about his wife?" I asked. "I mean, Mr. Dawson's wife. She didn't want them either?"

"She died," Ruben said, "two months before they were supposed to leave Peru."

Before I left, Ruben offered to give me one book from the collection. I chose the one I'd had in my hand earlier. Ruben said I should date it like Dawson did, so I went to the last page of the book and wrote down today's date, my name, and *Oudenburg*.

The brochure of the school Marie recommended has been sitting on the table since Saturday. I looked at it while thinking, *Maybe Marie was right.* Maybe Father could stay like he wanted, and maybe Father would change his personality and improve his social life. But maybe was not good enough. I needed something more concrete than maybe.

I called Father and suggested we take Mother's stuff down to *De Kringwinkel* today. Father said they could do a pick-up free of charge, so there was no need for us to do the drop-off. I ignored this information and asked Father to be ready in half an hour.

While Father went back into the house to look for the address of *De Kringwinkel,* I put the two boxes in the trunk. Upon our departure Father offered to drive, but I refused. When I was little, we often drove without the company of music. Father couldn't bear any sound while driving. I remember even my discreet humming was too loud. Today I was impressed. We listened to two whole songs before Father asked to switch off the radio. But I didn't get to enjoy the music much since I was wondering the whole time when Father would reinstate the silence.

"How come there are only two boxes?" I asked. "I thought there were already three boxes just for Mother's clothes."

"I made some changes," Father replied.

"Did you have to make an appointment with the people from *De Kringwinkel?*"

"No," Father answered. "You only make appointments when you need them to do the pick-up. Why?"

"Good," I said. "Then we can afford a little detour."

"What detour?" Father asked suspiciously.

I pointed out the school brochure in the glove compartment and told him that was what the detour was for.

"You tricked me," Father said unhappily.

"Technically I didn't. I really wanted to help with the *Kringwinkel* thing, but I just thought we could visit the school first."

Father didn't react. He was looking out the window.

"Marie recommended it," I said. "I told her you wanted to stay. She thought it might help."

"Help what?"

"What do you think?" I said. "Help you learn to speak the

language."

Father browsed through the brochure and read one of the headings out loud:

Anderstaligen die Nederlands kunnen spreken, integreren zich sneller.

"And this doesn't sound like propaganda to you?" Father questioned.

"Not to me, it doesn't," I said. "Not if you're planning on living the rest of your life here."

Father closed the brochure, and the silence plotted its way back into the car. I pulled over on the street opposite the school gate. Father requested to go in alone. There were a few groups of students chattering by the building. I guessed they were having a break. From the look of the students, the school seemed quite multicultural and had a wide age range. At that very moment, I thought this might work.

I watched Father go through the gate and into the building, out of sight. Rebecca called, asking if my detour plan had worked. I told her we were still in the middle of it. Shortly after, I saw Father walk out of the building and come to a halt in the middle of the entrance square. Father hardly moved. He just stood there staring at the students. Then suddenly, without having spoken to anyone, he walked out of the school gate. I was very confused, so I got out when he approached the car.

"What happened?" I asked, baffled.

Father walked past me and got into the car without responding to my question. I got into the car and asked him again. Father complained about the atmosphere of the school and mentioned that he didn't appreciate ethnic teachers teaching Flemish.

"What? Please tell me you're joking," I said and started the car. "This is preposterous."

"I need someone local."

"How do you know they're not?" I said. "Besides, that shouldn't even be an issue."

"I just mean I prefer someone local," Father said. "I'm not implying anything."

"And by local you mean someone who is white," I stated.

I felt offended. I'd never expected Father to be one of them.

"Anyway," I continued, though still feeling upset, "they must have local Flemish teachers too." I looked at Father. "Stop making all these excuses."

Father didn't respond anymore. Before we reached *De Kringwinkel*, I told him that the school was a test. And regardless of his so-called legitimate concern, the whole thing was a disappointment. Father didn't just prove to me, but also to himself, that if he stayed he would be eaten alive by all these conflicts and frustrations. He looked at me and told me to drive back to the house. No *Kringwinkel* today. Father said he needed to go through the boxes again.

I was checking the date of our return flight when I realized that today was our ten-year anniversary. I made some excuses and drove to *Brugge*. Two hours later, I came back with ten old-fashioned chapstick cases made of tin. It was a miracle that I found them in a store that sold military accessories. Rebecca was pleased with the gift. While I was out, Rebecca went to pick up something from Sarah. Apparently she had ordered something after the baking event. It was a cheesecake. Mother used to make cheesecakes on her and Father's anniversaries.

Since I can remember, every year for their anniversary, Mother would make a cheesecake. Father would be in a good mood before he even woke up and stayed excited the entire day just for a taste of Mother's cheesecake after dinner. I helped Mother make the cake once, and it didn't looked like something really special to me. Every ingredient was easy to get, such as cream cheese, sugar, vanilla, salt, eggs and lemon zest. For the crust there would be butter, more sugar and graham crackers. And on top of that, Mother followed recipes. Father explained that though everyone could follow recipes, because it came from Mother, it harbored a unique taste. Father used to say that it was where the magic of love lived. I always giggled when Father said that with a straight face. I knew the cheesecake in front of me came from Sarah, but as crazy as it might sound, it tasted just like Mother's.

I told Rebecca that we should properly thank Marie for being so understanding towards Father's episode in her store. Rebecca thought it was a great idea. She said we could invite her to Father's place and she would cook. I called Marie and asked her over to Father's house for dinner on Saturday evening. Marie sounded a bit preoccupied, but she accepted the invitation and told me she looked forward to Rebecca's cooking.

Father, surprisingly, didn't object to the dinner idea. It seemed to me that Father didn't dislike Marie. I could see why. The fact that some of her features were similar to Mother helped. I realized this last time when I had a talk with Marie at Sokoke. Both Mother and Marie were quite petite, though I think Mother was a little taller. Both had long, dark brown hair hanging over their shoulders, though Marie's hair was slightly wavier than Mother's. Both were blessed with sunny bright smiles and both possessed that natural charm of West Flemish women. If I could see it, Father probably saw it too.

We went to a Thai restaurant just outside *Izegem* in the evening. I found it in one of the restaurant guides that was lying on a table next to the reception. It was a bit of a drive, but I thought we should do something nice for the anniversary, just the three of us. The name of the restaurant was Pinto Thai. We had a Thai restaurant back in West Village, New York, with the same name, but the Pinto Thai here had a more authentic atmosphere. According to the hostess, the restaurant was opened three years ago by a West Flemish lady and her husband, who was a Thai chef.

After our wonderful dinner, we were introduced to the owners, Stephanie and Jaturong. They were a young couple, both in their thirties. They met in Bangkok five years ago when Stephanie was over there working for a British company. Jaturong was a chef at a restaurant Stephanie often visited for business dinners. One evening, a client Stephanie was hosting complained about the food and insisted on seeing the chef. That was how the two of them met for the first time. Stephanie said she knew there was nothing wrong with the food and was utterly embarrassed by the client's behavior, so she went back to apologize the next day. After accepting her apology and a bottle of twelve-year-old Japanese whiskey, Jaturong asked Stephanie out. They got married the year after. Four years ago, when Stephanie was made redundant, she persuaded Jaturong to move to Belgium and open his own restaurant. Stephanie said, "Thank god the restaurant plan worked out," or she would have felt so guilty for dragging a talented chef away from his success after years of hard work. I noticed Jaturong stroking Stephanie's back when she told the story. I guessed it was his way of comforting his wife. Jaturong said they were happy with their life here, especially with the twins on the way. I looked at Jaturong and thought, *If only Father was half as social as him.*

While waiting for our coats, Stephanie handed us what looked like a dessert box and wished us a happy anniversary. Inside there was a cheesecake. Rebecca and I looked at each other and smiled. I took a bite, and it tasted just like Mother's.

Being married to a perfectionist like Rebecca is no picnic. I have been out since nine running errands and getting the groceries for tonight, while Rebecca cleaned and set up the dining room in Father's house. Rebecca decided to make tomato pies and Moros y Cristianos. She wanted to show Marie the American, especially New Jersey, takes on Italian and Cuban food. Personally, I adore Rebecca's Moros y Cristianos.

Later, after my help in the kitchen was rejected, I went to check on Jimmy. I was surprised he wasn't hogging the TV. Rebecca said Jimmy had followed Father upstairs half an hour ago. As I approached the second floor, I heard indistinct voices. Father was in the bedroom talking with Jimmy. I stopped by the door and saw they were sitting on the bed with a box in between them.

"What's in here?" Jimmy asked and pointed at the box.

"Videotapes your Grandma Anne made," Father replied.

"Grandma Anne made videos? Was she an actress?"

Father laughed. "No, silly Jimmy, she was not, but if she was, she would have been the prettiest."

Jimmy took one tape out of the box. "Can I watch Grandma Anne?"

I could see Father was uncertain whether it was appropriate to show Mother's videos to Jimmy, but Jimmy kept on asking with no signs of giving up. Father slid the tape into the player and pressed play. I hadn't seen this video before, so I stayed by the door and watched. Mother was standing in front of a white wall, like the one I saw last time, but this time Mother was wearing a long-sleeved cream blouse and a green knee-length skirt. The blouse had some finely patterned lace sewn on the collar. Mother's talk, except for a few details here and there, was almost identical to the one I saw last. Jimmy commented that Mother looked young and so beautiful in the video. This must be one of the early ones Mother recorded. I spotted Father's eyes locked on the digital presence of Mother, and his lips were attempting to mouth her name. Like last time, the video ended with Mother talking about her concerns and wishes regarding Father's life after her. Father stopped the video and took out the tape.

"Why was Grandma Anne so worried about you?" Jimmy asked.

"Grandma Anne worried too much," Father said. "Grandpa is fine."

"Then why do you look sad?"

"Well," Father said, "Grandma Anne just passed away. Of course Grandpa is sad."

"But you also look sad in those photos of you and Grandma Anne downstairs in the living room," Jimmy said.

"Do I?" Father asked and looked startled by Jimmy's observation.

Jimmy nodded.

"Well, you got me there. Grandpa didn't realize he looked sad in the photo."

"Do you want me to kiss your nose so you're not sad anymore?" Jimmy asked.

"Where did you learn that?" Father asked, looking surprised.

"Daddy said Grandma Anne used to do that when you and Daddy were sad."

Father patted Jimmy on the head and let Jimmy kiss his nose. Three times, as Mother would have done.

"Are you coming to live with us in New York?" Jimmy asked.

"Do you think Grandpa should?" Father answered with a question.

"Daddy said it would be better for you. He said Grandma Anne also thought it would be better for you."

"Your daddy said that, huh," Father said.

Jimmy nodded.

I walked into the room when Father got up to move the box off the bed. I told Father I heard their conversation. I then pulled the a-grandson-needs-his-grandfather cliché on Father, trying to convince him, again, to move back with us. Father didn't seem very happy that I brought this issue up repeatedly. He said nothing and walked out of the room.

The doorbell rang at eight o'clock sharp. Marie arrived with a bottle of red wine and thanked us for inviting her. She was wearing a grey-purple summer jacket with a waistband tied at the front shaping her figure nicely, and underneath it a yellow blouse and a pair of jeans completed the outfit. On this evening in late February, Marie looked like she was one season ahead of us.

Before heading into the dining room, Rebecca lined us up in the hallway, and we listened to the menu for tonight. I guaranteed Marie she would not be disappointed. There were place cards indicating where everyone was supposed to sit. Rebecca had turned Father's dining room into one of those fancy ones in some period drama. Looking at my NYU sweatshirt, I suddenly felt underdressed. After we were seated, Marie asked Father about the purpose of his visit to her store the other day. Father said it was nothing important.

Rebecca served the dinner and we ate quietly. I must have still been upset about Father's earlier reaction upstairs. I couldn't seem to bring myself to engage in the conversation with a good temper. Soon it was obvious that I was a mood-killer tonight at the table, and it became official when I told Marie that Father had agreed to move back with us to New York. Of course Father hadn't agreed to anything of the sort, but the words just came out of my mouth. Though he didn't say a single word, I knew Father was furious. He got up and withdrew from the dining room. I was embarrassed that Marie had to witness my obscene behavior, so I excused myself and followed Father out of the dining room.

I found him smoking under the skylight at the end of the hallway upstairs. The moonlight tonight sculpted two shadows of him.

"You can't keep avoiding it, Father," I said as I walked towards him.

"Would you just stop cornering me already," Father said and exhaled a thin line of white smoke out of the skylight.

"You think I like it?" I said. "I don't enjoy being a bad cop, Father, especially not when I know I'm doing the right thing."

"What's so horrible about me staying here?"

"Uh, being totally alone, maybe? Or, in your case, dying out here and nobody knowing."

"I'll learn the language, and I'll start talking to people," Father said.

"How?" I raised my voice a bit. "You didn't even talk to anyone who came to Mother's funeral, except that speech I asked you to do. And you know what, this is not just about the language anymore."

"What then?" Father also raised his voice a bit.

"It's about you not being able to show people in town that

you want to be with them. And it's about you not being recognized as one of them because of your lack of social interest in them."

"What makes you think I'm not interested?" Father asked.

"I don't know and nobody knows," I said, looking him in the eye. "And that's the problem, Father. You've got to show people that you care if you don't want to end up alone."

"Fine. So I will."

"No, Father, I don't think you even believe that yourself," I was nearly yelling. "You didn't do it the last forty-three years, and you're not going to do it now. You couldn't even get past those lousy excuses you made and give that school a try!"

"And you think," Father stated in a dubious tone, "all my fear for social interaction will just magically disappear once I move back with you?"

"I'm not saying that. But at the very least, you'd be with us."

Father's cigarette was nearly out. The ash fell through his fingers and landed on the floor. The conversation again ended without any apparent progress, but I somehow sensed that I had made my case stronger tonight. I realized it was way past Jimmy's bedtime, so I left Father to his thoughts and went downstairs. Rebecca and Marie were drinking and chatting in the living room, and Jimmy was next to them watching cartoons. I turned off the TV and took Jimmy upstairs.

After reading Jimmy four bedtime stories, I fell asleep with him in my old bed again. And like the last time, it was a little crammed but it was fine.

Meubel Galerie Vynckier was written big and bold on the wall of a creamy-yellow brick bungalow behind *Huize Rossetti. What an unusual use of color,* I thought. The bungalow didn't seem to be inhabited and the sign appeared to be just an advertisement. I was amazed that I only noticed this veranda-less bungalow tonight. It reminded me of South Bend, Indiana.

Mother said that after I was born, we moved from downtown to the northwest side of the city, close to all the factories, distribution centers and the airport. I don't remember much about South Bend since I only lived the first year of my life there, but the sound of airplane engines zooming and the image of snow falling across the sky were vivid even to a one - year-old.

On Christmas Eve, 1969, I was running a fever since afternoon, and around ten o'clock when my temperature didn't drop as the doctor had predicted on the telephone, Father decided to wrap me up with thick blankets and drive me to the emergency room. From our house to the Memorial Hospital of South Bend, it was about seven kilometers straight through the Lincoln Way West. When we were about four kilometers away from the hospital, the car broke down. Father immediately got out of the car and continued carrying me to the hospital on foot. It was nearly minus eight degrees that evening, but he had rushed out of the house with only a T-shirt on. The cold air and the snow were slowing Father down. I can vaguely recall his accelerating heartbeats and the heavy panting. Soon Father's hands were frozen and his toes were numb, so he went knocking on the doors of the houses by the side of the road. A twenty-something African-American woman from a brick bungalow came out onto her porch while Father was trying to get help from the house next door.

"Are you looking for the Hendersons?" the woman yelled. "They're out of town."

Father ran to her and explained that I needed urgent medical attention. The woman fetched her car keys and drove us to the hospital. The doctor told Father it was fortunate that I arrived when I did. Any later I could have died. The woman's name was Tracey Williams. Mrs. Williams was my lifesaver, and later became my godmother. Unlike most godparents who get to watch their godchildren grow up, Mrs. Williams could only see me in pictures Mother sent her after we moved more than six thousand kilometers away.

I remember it was on my fifth birthday that Mother showed me a framed photograph of Mrs. Williams. In it, Mrs. Williams was wearing a typical sixties shirtwaist dress in tropical colors and a well-crafted bouffant hairdo. Mrs. Williams was very fashionable. In the short time she and Mother spent together, she gave Mother lots of fashion tips. Mother used to say, and she said it proudly, that before Mrs. Williams, she didn't even know women actually slept with Coke-can-sized rollers in their hair every night, just so they could achieve the bouffant hairstyle.

Throughout the years, in her letters, Mrs. Williams talked about her son, Edward, a lot. Edward was two years younger than me. He was a straight-A student, polite, ambitious and a charmer. Edward was a good old American boy, and Mrs. Williams was very proud of him. When I was a freshman at NYU, during the spring break, I finally visited Mrs. Williams for the very first time after she saved my life on that particular evening. She offered to pick me up at the airport, and she recognized me the second I exited the arrival gate. The reunion was extraordinary. I then learned that Mrs. Williams hadn't been Mrs. Williams for years. Mrs. Williams wished to keep it secret, so she never told Mother about the divorce. She told me I could call her Tracey, but I suggested *Aunt Tracey*.

Edward arrived a day later. He was probably the only person, other than myself, who didn't go on some crazy trip with their peers that spring break. Although it was the first time I ever met Edward, there were no extra bedrooms in the house, so Aunt Tracey put him and me in the same room. I couldn't tell if Edward was cool about this arrangement, but for me, I didn't mind.

Edward's appearance was expressive and up-to-date. The first thing I spotted when he came through the door was his long, straight, bleached hair. I was surprised and at the same time fascinated. I didn't know black people could grow such hair. I learned later that the hair was not real. When Aunt Tracey introduced me to him, Edward walked straight into his room without sparing me a glance. Later that evening I found him, without a shirt on, sitting by the bedroom window, smoking a joint. With the moonlight beating down on his face and torso, Edward looked a bit like John Baxter Taylor. I walked into the room and began to unpack.

"Mother said you're studying at NYU?" Edward asked.

"Yes," I said and turned to Edward briefly before I continued to unpack. "I'm a freshman."

"What's your major?" Edward asked and puffed on the joint. He continued before I could answer his question. "I'd like to live in New York City too."

"You would?" I asked. "Why?"

"I want to go to the New York Academy of Art."

"You're an artist?"

"No," Edward said, "no one is actually."

"Okay. So why go there if you don't want to be an artist?"

"I didn't say I don't want to be an artist," Edward explained. "I just don't think anybody can actually be one."

"Okay," I said.

Edward raised his arm and offered me his joint. I refused at first, but Edward was quite persistent, and so I caved. Prior to that day, I had never smoked anything. Not even cigarettes. The effect was overwhelming. My heart started pounding really fast and my throat was getting dry. He sneered when I returned the joint to him. I watched Edward finish it by himself. He threw the roach out of the window, and then he got up and announced it was time for a shower.

Aunt Tracey prepared a one-person mattress for me on the floor by the foot of Edward's bed. The mattress was too thin for my liking, so I couldn't find a comfortable spot to fall asleep on. Five minutes after Edward switched off the lights, my back started to hurt, so I moved around a lot. All the noise I caused must have annoyed Edward. He sat up in his bed and asked what my problem was. He was irritated. I explained and told him that maybe I should go downstairs and sleep on the sofa. Edward didn't think it was a good idea because he thought it would be dreadful for Aunt Tracey to find out that her guest had slept on the sofa. He said I shouldn't be selfish.

"Selfish?" I said. "What are you talking about? My back is really hurting, and I don't mind sleeping on the sofa. I can explain to Aunt Tracey tomorrow morning. I'm sure she would understand."

"You don't know Mother as well as I do," Edward said.

"So what am I supposed to do?"

Edward thought about it for a moment. "You can come sleep in the bed."

"With you?" I asked.

"What do you think?" Edward said. "You're not suggesting that I sleep on that crappy mattress, are you?"

"But your bed is not big enough," I said observantly.

"Well," Edward tried to make his case, "either this or you can stay down there and have back pain for a week, or worse, you can go sleep on the sofa and be an ungrateful guest to your hostess. Your call."

Edward would make a great lawyer. I went to the bed and lay down next to him. The bed was indeed a bit small for two grown men, but my back felt an instant change of comfort. We were lying next to each other with only ten centimeters between our shoulders. Edward fell asleep before me. A few minutes later, he stretched in his sleep, and his right arm landed on my chest. I didn't want to wake him, so I didn't react. I remained in that position until I fell asleep eventually.

The next morning, I talked about the mattress with Aunt Tracey, and as I had predicted, she didn't take it personally and borrowed a better mattress from her neighbor.

The last time I ran into Edward was in a pizzeria two blocks away from where I worked. I was grabbing a quick bite alone when I saw him come through the door with a little girl. We were both surprised to see one another and greeted each other with a hug. He introduced me to his four-year-old daughter, Jasmine, and we talked for a while. Edward's dream had come true. He went to the New York Academy of Art and afterwards became a teacher there. He looked very happy.

I had finished my pizza when Edward's wife, Johanna, came in. I gave her my greetings and then excused myself. After I walked out of the pizzeria, I turned around to wave at Edward and his family. I saw Edward raise his arm like he did that night, but there was no joint between his fingers – only his open palm waving.

The weather forecast on the morning radio said that it would be sunny, though possibly windy, all day today. I was making tea and heating milk for Rebecca and Jimmy when I thought of taking a day trip to the coast. I rang Father around noon and suggested the idea to him.

"It would be like a family trip," I said. Father was reluctant at first, but later agreed after I'd granted his wish to be the driver for the day. At a quarter to one, we were on the road.

After stating that we must be the only people who chose to go to the coast on this cold and windy day in February, Father devoted his attention to the driving and didn't say a word before we arrived in *Blankenberge.* It was quite amusing to see Father drive again. I noticed him reach for the cigarettes in his shirt pocket a couple of times, but each time he stopped short. I assumed it was because Jimmy was in the car. Rebecca patted me on my shoulder from the back seat. She was trying to say that this unplanned excursion was a good idea. I remembered that whenever we had family trips, though really not that many, I always requested to sit in the passenger seat, and Mother always let me despite Father's concern. But before we departed, Father would move me to the back seat to sit with Mother. He thought it was safer that way for all of us. I wondered, if there was more room in the back seat, would Father have ordered me to sit in the back like he always did?

The GPS was not on. Father seemed confident in finding the correct route without receiving any extra guidance. Not even from me apparently. Father told me to quit stressing him out after I tried to tell him that he had gotten off at the wrong exit.

After arriving in *Blankenberge,* we drove through the town heading towards the beach. Father was right, there were only a few small groups of people strolling through the streets. The town looked very different to the one I remembered. It seemed like so much had changed. But of course, we never visited the coast during the wintertime. Looking out the car window, I wondered how this beautiful coastal town became such a breeding ground for modern apartment blocks. These tall buildings were all built next to one another, facing the sea, and they endeavored to portray a luxurious lifestyle of living by the beach. I couldn't help but ponder whether or not the local people were pleased with what they had accomplished.

Then again, it was probably never desirable to prevent the old from being replaced by the new.

We soon parked the car and walked down a boardwalk to the beach. It was sunny, but the wind made it cold. Father never really liked beaches and the sea. He only took us to the coast because Mother adored everything about it. If I remember correctly, Father can't even swim. Well, not that I'm any better. I barely made it through swim class in school. Mother used to joke that if Father and I were drowning at the same time she could probably only save one person, so we should never go into the sea together.

Unlike Father, I loved going to the coast. And I always looked forward to feeling the sand being washed away from the bottom of my feet. One summer, when I was five, Mother rented a blow-up rubber boat. I was overjoyed and hopped right into it. I don't remember all the details about what happened on the boat that day, but Mother told me that she left me on the boat for one second to go and get the sunblock. The next thing she knew, I was already a hundred meters away from the shore. Luckily, shortly after, the current started bringing me back. But when I was about twenty meters away from the beach, a wave flipped my boat over, and I was swallowed by the sea. Fortunately I was only underwater for a brief moment, and the wave soon rolled me ashore. The whole thing happened quite fast, so before Mother and Father had the time to realize what was going on, I was already saved. I was lying on the beach with my body fully covered in sand when they rushed to me in horror. They were worried sick, but according to Mother, I was smiling. And that was the first and the last time I have ever been on a rubber boat.

Father was holding Jimmy's hand as we walked down the beach. I slowed down and asked Father to watch Jimmy for a while so that Rebecca and I could enjoy some alone time. Before we parted ways, we agreed to meet back by the car around four.

I first took Rebecca for a long walk in the city, and then I showed her the *vuurtoren* where the wedding photo of Mother and Father was taken. The building seemed taller in the picture, but its nineteen-fifties architectural lines made a better impression in reality. We took a selfie in front of the tower before heading back.

Jimmy was sitting on the roof of the car eating ice cream from a cone when Rebecca and I arrived. Father was standing in front of him, also with an ice cream cone. After Jimmy finished, Rebecca took him into the car because the wind was getting stronger. Father and I stayed outside for a cigarette.

"We were at the lighthouse just now," I said.

"How was it?" Father asked. "It's been years since I was there."

"It was okay. Hasn't changed much."

I showed the selfie we took. Father commented on the angle. He thought we could have held the camera a bit higher.

"And you?" I asked. "What did you and Jimmy do?"

"We just walked around the beach, and then he asked for ice cream, so we went and got some."

"It's crazy, isn't it?" I said. "How they eat ice cream all year long here."

"It's not that crazy. You used to beg for ice cream in winter too."

I turned and looked at Father. The wrinkles around his eyes crinkled when the wind blew in his face. Suddenly, convincing Father to move to New York felt like too ambitious a task. But he proved me wrong.

"I'm coming to New York with you," Father said.

"What? Really?" I asked incredulously.

"Yes. I'll come and live with you, if you'll still have me of course."

"Sure," I said. "Yes, of course, sure, absolutely."

This turn of events nearly blew me away. I was speechless the entire ride back home. Father said it shouldn't take him longer than a month to arrange all the paperwork, and after everything was taken care of he would fly to New York on his own. I told Father we should inform Marie, but Father wished to keep it quiet.

For what reasons, I'm not sure.

Later in the evening when I was reading bedtime stories to little Jimmy, he told me what had happened when he was alone with Father in the afternoon. He said that after they had walked up and down the beach three times, he saw a girl sitting on a bench eating ice cream, so he asked Father for some. Father then took Jimmy to a store that sold ice cream, and as soon as they entered the store, a very old lady began to talk to Father.

"Was she speaking English?" I asked.

"No," Jimmy said. "She was speaking a funny language."

"Flemish?"

"I don't know," Jimmy said and covered his face with his palms. "I didn't understand."

"Did Grandpa Jeff talk to the old lady?" I asked.

Jimmy said Father stood in front of the lady without saying a word for a while, and he felt Father's hand trembling. Then the old lady turned to Jimmy, smiled and said a few words to him. But Jimmy didn't understand, so he quickly hid behind Father.

"And then Grandpa Jeff was going to leave without getting the ice cream," Jimmy said, sounding whiny.

"He was? And then what happened?"

"I made a sad face," Jimmy said guiltily.

"You did?" I said and laughed.

Jimmy said his strategy worked because Father turned back to the old lady and spoke.

"Grandpa Jeff talked to the old lady?" I asked and tried to disguise the excitement in my voice.

"Yes," Jimmy said.

"What did Grandpa Jeff say?"

"I don't know," Jimmy said and again covered his face with his palms. "Grandpa Jeff was also speaking funny."

If what Jimmy said was true, Father had possibly spoken Flemish to the old lady. I was astonished by this story. I explored hundreds of thousands of scenarios in my head, hoping to track down some logic behind the sudden revelation about Father, but I failed to find one that made sense.

Before I fell asleep, with my eyes closed, I recalled Father's face from this afternoon when he told me he wanted to come back to the States. I studied every muscle in it and saw no signs of compromise. Not one bit.

Father has been busy working in the garage the past three months, ever since he moved back to live with us in New York. During the weekdays, I see Father head to the garage at nine in the morning, and when I come home from work in the evening, he is still in there. On the weekends, I hear the sounds of all kinds of machinery coming from the garage. It must be a project of some sort, I think. Father won't allow anyone to know what is going on, but he promised that in two days we could park our cars back in the garage again. I have been ignoring my curiosity up until now, but today something drove me to spy on Father. So after he went into the garage around ten to nine, I decided to peep through the garage window.

The garage looked like a small studio for photographers. There were two stage lights on poles standing in the middle of the room facing a big wooden panel that was painted white and nailed to the wall. In between the lights and the panel stood a video camera on a tripod. After switching on the lights, Father went to a corner looking focused, and began, what seemed to me, like rehearsing. Father sat in a chair with some paper in his hand, and he mouthed the words as if he was trying to memorize a script. I looked around the production Father had set up in the garage and thought that whatever this was for, he deserved a medal for such determination. I was in the middle of admiring his efforts when Father put down the paper and made his way to the set. He pressed a button on the side of the camera and then went in front of it. For fifteen minutes, Father stood there in his blazer with the suede elbow pads and recorded a speech. The garage window was shut, so I couldn't hear what Father was saying, but he seemed nervous yet confident at the same time. It was odd.

At dinner, Father announced that starting Wednesday, he would be teaching English twice a week at the local community college. It's an evening program designed for elderly immigrants. The principal went to the same high school as Father. Although she never really knew Father, according to her, his writings spoke right to her heart. So when she ran into him the other day in the drugstore, she recruited him.

"It's just to help out, nothing serious," he said. But later in the evening, I saw him ironing his shirts and polishing his leather shoes.

Father asked me to drive him to the post office tomorrow when I offered to take his blazer to the dry cleaner. He said he wanted to post something to Marie. *That something must be the video he recorded,* I thought. My curiosity was killing me. I needed to see the video tonight before Father posted it. I waited until everyone was sound asleep to sneak into the garage. The moonlight provided some visibility, so I left the lights off. And also, I didn't want to attract any attention. But while I was trying to get my bearings, I knocked over a few empty tin cans. I felt like an amateur burglar.

The video camera was a very old model from JVC that worked with VHS tapes. I was amazed to see such an outdated machine still functioning. I was hesitating to take the tape out because I wasn't sure if we even had a VHS player in the house to play it, when I heard footsteps approaching. I put the camera back on the tripod and hid behind the broken refrigerator. It was Father. He entered the garage carrying a flashlight in his mouth as his hands were holding a small television and a VHS player. Father quickly connected those two electronics and began to play back the video he had recorded.

In the video, Father spoke the dialect from Mother's town. He stammered, and his accent was as absurd as could be, but Father, word for word, finished the speech. It was an ordinary thank-you message, really, but Father managed to turn it into a tear-jerking performance.

After Father went back into the house, I stayed and watched the video again and again. Each time I thought of Mother, and I imagined her giving Father three kisses on the nose.

CHRONOLOGY

DATE	LIFE	HISTORICAL EVENTS
1947	Anne Vermeersch is born in West Flanders, Belgium, on October 10 to Luc Vermeersch & Lieve Van den Weghe.	
1953	Vermeersch enters primary school.	28 people die in the North Sea flood in Belgium.
1956		262 miners die in a fire in a coal mine in Marcinelle, Belgium.
1957	Lieve Van den Weghe dies.	The Treaty of Rome establishes the European Economic Community between Belgium, Italy, West Germany, France, the Netherlands and Luxembourg.
1958		King Baudouin officially opens the World Fair (Expo '58) in Brussels.
1959	Vermeersch enters secondary school.	Prince Albert marries Italian princess Paola Ruffo di Calabria.
1960		King Baudouin marries Doña Fabiola de Mora y Aragón.
1961		73 people die in a Sabena Boeing 707 crash near Brussels, including the entire United States figure skating team and coaches.

1962		Belgium reestablishes diplomatic relations with the Congo.
1963		The language border in Belgium is established. This will become the foundation for the further federalization of the country.
1964	Vermeersch travels to Amsterdam during the Easter Holidays.	
1965	Vermeersch graduates from secondary school.	Bob Dylan releases the album *Highway 61 Revisited.*
1966		NATO decides to move SHAPE headquarters to Belgium.
1967	Vermeersch studies at the School of Social Work at Indiana University (South Bend), USA.	
1968	Vermeersch marries Jeff Brown.	Delphine Boël, illegitimate daughter of King Albert II, is born.
1969	Vermeersch's son, Jonathan, is born.	Willy Brandt becomes the Chancellor of West Germany.
1970	Vermeersch gives up her scholarship. The Brown family moves back to West Flanders, Belgium.	

1971	Vermeersch begins working at the local city hall.	The US dollar floods the European currency market.
1972		Belgium hosts the European Football Championship.
1973		The Volvo automobile distribution center opens in Ghent, Belgium.
1974		Anne Sexton dies.
1975	Luc Vermeersch dies.	
1977	The Brown family sells the old house and moves to a remote area at the edge of town.	The European Patent Institute is founded. Karl Ristikivi dies. Vladimir Nabokov dies.
1978	Vermeersch begins a second profession as a freelance seamstress.	
1980		The second State reform takes place in Belgium.
1983		Prince Charles of Belgium dies.
1985		39 Juventus fans die in the *Heizeldrama* in the Heysel Stadium in Brussels.
1986		*J'aime la vie* by Sandra Kim wins the Eurovision Song Contest for Belgium.

1987	Vermeersch's son leaves for New York, USA.	180 people drown in the Zeebrugge ferry disaster.
1989		The Berlin Wall falls.
1990	Vermeersch's son studies at NYU with a full scholarship.	
1994	Vermeersch's son graduates from NYU.	Richard Nixon dies.
1995	Vermeersch is made department coordinator at the city hall.	The Schengen Agreement is established.
1996		Marc Dutroux, a Belgian serial killer, is arrested for the third time.
1997		Diana, Princess of Wales, dies.
2000	Vermeersch stops working as a seamstress.	
2001		The Third Millennium begins.
2003	Vermeersch's son marries Rebecca Walker.	
2004		Marlon Brando dies.

2005	Vermeersch's first grandson, Jimmy, is born. Vermeersch visits her son and his family in New York, USA.	
2007	Vermeersch has her first heart attack.	
2009	Vermeersch retires and begins to receive a pension.	Herman Van Rompuy, Prime Minister of Belgium, is designated the first permanent President of the European Council.
2011	Vermeersch has a second heart attack.	7 people are killed in a murder-suicide attack in Liège, Belgium.
2013	Anne Vermeersch dies in West Flanders, Belgium, on February 4.	

GEMEENTELIJKE FICHE 01-01-2011

Waregem	933/35660	Diksmuide	201/16166
Brugge	4060/112817	Houthulst	87/9560
Kortrijk	4328/70533	Langemark-Poelkapelle	111/7737
Beernem	190/15029	Izegem	516/26728
Damme	182/10665	Ardooie	170/8890
Knokke-Heist	1749/32242	Lichtervelde	110/8385
Roeselare	1942/56196	Deerlijk	177/11109
Ledegem	118/9461	Harelbeke	679/26082
Wevelgem	513/30561	Ingelmunster	276/10404
Koksijde	751/21213	Tielt	515/19207
Lo-Reninge	36/3282	Wingene	190/13706
De Panne	835/9896	Zedelgem	259/22096
Veurne	182/11367	Oostrozebeke	110/7421
Alveringem	79/4868	Dentergem	116/8196
Vleteren	45/3672	Pittem	160/6562
Wielsbeke	171/9005	Blankenberge	718/18379
Meulebeke	236/10833	Jabbeke	177/13507
Avelgem	170/9490	De Haan	414/12110
Zwevegem	359/23737	Staden	121/10865
Anzegem	111/14221	Middelkerke	413/18468
Ichtegem	149/13710	Nieuwpoort	324/11058
Oostende	4393/65337	Zuienkerke	34/2730
Gistel	201/11581	Ruiselede	121/5088
Menen	2619/30117	Oostkamp	304/22231
Wervik	906/19577	Koekelare	74/8390
Moorslede	125/10733	Hooglede	155/9812
Lendelede	64/5583	Kortemark	100/12074
Kuurne	473/12490	Ieper	1116/33978
Spiere-Helkijn	112/2015	Mesen	136/812
Torhout	346/19634	Heuvelland	530/7470
Bredene	422/15962	Poperinge	405/19577
Oudenburg	102/8941	Zonnebeke	139/12169